HOLLY HOMICIDE
A HOLIDAY COZY MYSTERY
BOOK ELEVEN

TONYA KAPPES

TONYA KAPPES
WEEKLY NEWSLETTER

Want a behind-the-scenes journey of me as a writer? The ups and downs, new deals, book sales, giveaways and more? I share it all! Join the exclusive Southern Sleuths private group today! Go to www.patreon.com/Tonyakappesbooks

As a special thank you for joining, you'll get an exclusive copy of my cross-over short story, *A CHARMING BLEND*. Go to Tonyakappes.com and click on subscribe at the top of the home page.

CHAPTER ONE

Jingle, jingle, jingle. The soft, rhythmic sounds of jingle bells caught my ear, a sweet, familiar tune that blended seamlessly with the merry chatter drifting up from the streets below.

The merriment outside my apartment window fluttered in through the slightly open pane, brushing past the chilly breeze that kissed my cheeks. I was fully immersed in meeting a deadline for the *Junction Journal*. The pressure was causing me to sweat, a feeling I despised. Sweating was for summer, and I much preferred the crisp, clean cold of winter.

The hint of fresh, wintry air tickled my skin, refreshing my mind and providing a small escape from the flickering cursor on my screen. Outside, the holiday cheer seemed to pour from every corner of Holiday Junction, bringing with it the sounds of children laughing and the occasional hum of a Christmas tune. Snowflakes flurried through the gap in the window, landing softly on my desk like little winter messengers reminding me of the season's magic.

"And that's a wrap," I said to myself after typing the final keystrokes. The town's event schedule for tomorrow was ready. I sighed in relief after sending it, and that persistent jingle caught my attention once more.

Jingle, jingle, jingle. The bells sounded closer, the chimes mingling with rising oohs and aahs.

I glanced up from my laptop, a smile curling on my lips. The entire town had been buzzing for weeks, counting down to the grand opening of our month-long Christmas Market located on the lawn of the old Christmas Lodge on the far end of the art district.

The festival, which would culminate in the glamorous Mistletoe Masquerade Ball at Elysian Evergreens, turned the normally quiet town into a glowing holiday hub.

I closed my laptop and lifted up the window, and a blast of chilly air whooshed in, carrying with it the smells of pine and cinnamon, making my heart swell with Christmas joy. Below me, the magic of the season was in full swing.

A horse-drawn sleigh draped in garlands of holly

and twinkling fairy lights was making its way down the main street of the art district, its grand entrance casting a spell on everyone in its path. Two majestic black stallions pranced ahead of the sleigh body through the snow, their glossy coats glistening under the glow of the lanterns mounted on either side. The coachman, a dapper figure, sat tall and proud, his white-gloved hands gripping the reins. His top hat, flawlessly polished, gleamed each time he passed beneath one of the ornate carriage lights that lined the sidewalk.

Jingle, jingle, jingle. The collars around the horses' thick necks displayed large brass bells, and as the regal animals took each step, clear, melodic rings resounded through the streets like music from an old holiday movie.

Pedestrians bundled up in thick winter coats, colorful scarves, and knitted hats paused mid-step, enchanted by the scene. A little girl dressed in a bright-red coat with matching mittens clutched her mother's hand, her wide eyes reflecting the magic of the sleigh as she pointed excitedly toward the horses. Gleeful voices filled the air as all the other children tugged on their parents' coats, eager to follow the sleigh, which I was sure was going to the Christmas Market.

The first snow of the evening drifted down in

lazy, gentle flakes, blanketing the cobblestone streets in a soft layer of white. It was just enough to crunch underfoot, the kind of snow that made the world feel quiet and calm, as though time itself had slowed for that special moment.

The women in the crowd were a vision of holiday elegance—some in fur-trimmed muffs and woolen capes, their cheeks flushed from the cold, others sporting vibrant red and green scarves draped over coats lined with white fleece. The men wore thick gloves and wool hats pulled low over their ears, and friends clustered together, enjoying the smells of roasted chestnuts and spiced cider that lingered in the air, curling up from vendors set up along the sidewalk.

As the sleigh neared, the magic of the moment seemed to spread like the warmth of a crackling fire. The glow from the lanterns bathed the scene in a soft amber hue, casting long shadows across the street. Even the shops lining the sidewalk seemed to lean in closer, their windows glimmering with Christmas lights and festive displays of wreaths, candy canes, and handcrafted ornaments.

The coachman tipped his hat to the onlookers, his eyes twinkling with mischief as he snapped the reins ever so gently, encouraging the horses to lift their feet a little higher. The bells rang louder, announcing the sleigh's grand arrival in front of my apartment.

Jingle, jingle, jingle.

The crowd gasped softly as the sleigh slowed down.

The scene below was pure magic, a moment pulled straight from the pages of a holiday storybook.

"Whoa," the coachman called to the horses, bringing them to an abrupt stop just below my small balcony. The jingling of the bells ceased, and the crowd that had gathered watched in awe, their breath visible in the cold air.

I lifted the window fully this time, the chill sweeping into my cozy apartment and making me shiver. Grabbing the soft plaid blanket from my desk chair, I flung it around my shoulders, savoring the warmth before I leaned out to get a closer look. The sleigh stood grandly on the cobblestone street, the black stallions' exhales steaming as they pranced in place. I could see the coachman, still holding the reins, looking up at me with a knowing smile.

Curiosity got the better of me. I climbed carefully out the window that led out to my small balcony and peeked over the iron railing, looking beyond the empty flower boxes to see who might be stepping from the sleigh.

And then I saw him.

Darren Strickland, my boyfriend, emerged from behind the driver, his mussed-up brown hair catching the glow of the lanterns. His dark eyes locked on mine, and with a huge grin spread across his face, he waved up at me enthusiastically.

I pointed to myself, eyes widening, unsure if he really meant *me*.

Darren chuckled, shaking his head, then nodded vigorously.

"Yeah, you," he called up, his thick brows lifting in amusement as he gestured for me to come down. He gave another playful wave, the joy and mischief in his expression undeniable.

I couldn't help but laugh, my heart light and fluttering. Pedestrians, some still in the midst of their holiday shopping, paused to take in the scene. A few whispered to one another, speculating about what was happening, while others smiled, their cheeks rosy from the cold as they held cups of steaming cocoa or tucked gloved hands into the arms of their companions.

I waved back, excitement bubbling up inside me.

"Give me a minute," I called down before hurrying back through the window into the warmth of my apartment. My heart raced as I headed straight for my bedroom, but just as I reached for the doorknob, I realized I'd left the window wide open.

I spun around and retraced my steps, rushing to close it before all the heat escaped into the night. Before I had tugged it down halfway, I glanced out one more time to make sure I hadn't imagined the whole thing. Sure enough, there was Darren, still standing beside the sleigh, now leaning casually against the side with that ever-present grin of his, as though he had all the time in the world. He waved again, this time a little slower, and winked.

My heart officially melted. I quickly closed the window and scurried back to my bedroom, where I pulled on my thick woolen socks and my snow boots. The boots weren't glamorous, but they'd keep my feet warm in the snow. I hurriedly slipped into a cream-colored sweater and then threw on my long coat before grabbing a knitted scarf and gloves from the hallway closet on my way out the door.

The click of the door behind me echoed through the stairwell as I bounded down the steps, my boots tapping quickly against the wooden planks. I was breathing fast with excitement, and by the time I reached the bottom, the cold air hit me again like a brisk kiss from winter itself.

Darren was waiting for me beside the sleigh, his tall figure framed by the soft light of the streetlamps that made the snow around him shimmer. His dark eyes twinkled as he opened his arms wide, welcoming me.

"Surprise," he said, his voice warm and teasing as he helped me up into the sleigh. His hands, strong and sure, guided me as I stepped onto the wooden side and settled into the plush velvet seat.

Once I was in place, he pulled a thick, heavy blanket around my shoulders, tucking the corners snugly around me. The material was softer than I expected, and the warmth immediately spread through me, cutting through the chill in the air.

"I wanted to make sure you experienced the reopening of the Christmas Lodge," Darren said, leaning in close as he spoke, his breath misting between us. His voice was filled with affection, like he'd been planning this for a while. "It's been closed for years, and I know how much you've wanted to see it. I thought this would be the perfect way to kick off the season."

My heart swelled at his words, and I couldn't help but grin at the thought of what lay ahead. Everyone said the Christmas Lodge, a beloved part of Holiday Junction's history, had been a magical place before it closed down years ago, and apparently now it was reopening. I'd not heard that.

"I can't believe it," I said, wrapping my arms around his neck. "You've really outdone yourself."

He laughed, his eyes crinkling at the corners.

"Anything for you," he said and put his arm around me.

The sleigh jolted gently as the horses shifted, eager to be off. Darren took my gloved hand in his and gave it a soft squeeze as the coachman snapped the reins, and with the gentle jingle of the bells, we were off, gliding down the snow-covered street toward the Christmas Lodge.

The world around us felt like a snow globe, with snowflakes swirling in the air as we made our way through the festively decorated streets.

This month was going to be incredible.

CHAPTER TWO

The sleigh coasted its way past the bustling Christmas Market, and the glow of twinkling lights and the laughter of families faded into the distance behind us. With the clopping of hooves muffled by the fresh layer of snow, the horses pulled us up the winding path toward a place I hadn't visited but had come to know through stories. After decades of abandonment, the old Christmas Lodge had finally been purchased and restored for a grand reopening.

Darren glanced over at me, the grin still lingering on his lips.

"I thought you'd like this little detour," he said, squeezing my hand gently under the heavy blanket. "I know you've been curious about the lodge."

I couldn't help but smile, my breath catching in the cold night air. "I've heard so much about it lately.

Mama says it's booked for the next year, but knowing her, she's probably exaggerating." I snickered because there was no way Mama would know such a thing.

Darren chuckled, his breath fogging in the air between us. "Millie Kay and her gossip. Who knows, though? The place has quite the reputation already," he said.

As the sleigh crested the hill, the Christmas Lodge came into view, and I gasped.

It was nothing like I'd pictured.

The lodge was, in a word, magnificent. This was going to be the crown jewel of Holiday Junction, its recent restoration nothing short of a holiday miracle.

The sprawling structure seemed to sparkle from within, its enormous windows spilling warm golden light into the snow-covered courtyard that stretched out in front of it. Massive evergreen wreaths adorned with bright-red ribbons and twinkling lights hung from every window and door, their size so exaggerated I half-wondered if they'd been made for giants.

The building itself was constructed of sturdy timber and stone, giving it the feel of a grand chalet, with steep, snow-covered roofs that looked as though they had been plucked straight from a fairytale.

The entire edifice was dusted with fresh powder, making it glisten under the moonlight like it had been dipped in sugar. Icicles, long and perfectly formed, hung from the eaves, shimmering like delicate glass ornaments, each one catching the glow of the thousands of lights strung across the eaves along the outside of the lodge.

At the front stood an enormous Christmas tree towering proudly over even the tallest point of the lodge. The tree was decorated in true storybook fashion, decked out with garlands, giant baubles, and twinkling lights that looked like stars. At the very top, a crystal star sparkled so brightly that it could probably be seen from anywhere in the town below.

As we approached, I noticed that even the cobblestone pathway leading up to the entrance was lined with subtle lights embedded in the ground as if the earth itself had been enchanted for the season. Lanterns with flickering flames were carefully placed along the walkway, their glass etched with scenes of snowy villages and prancing reindeer.

"It's... it's even more beautiful than I imagined," I whispered, barely able to tear my eyes away from the spectacle in front of me.

"It's something, all right," Darren said, clearly amused by my awe. "Wait until you see the inside."

We glided closer, and I could see that the lodge was bustling with activity. The scene before me already looked like a Christmas postcard come to life.

Guests wrapped in luxurious coats and fur-trimmed hats milled about the front entrance, their laughter mingling as they sipped hot cocoa from delicate porcelain mugs. A doorman in a classic red uniform, complete with gold buttons and a black top hat, stood at the entrance, greeting guests with a warm smile and a tip of his hat.

"Mr. Strickland," the doorman said, "nice to see you and Ms. Rhinehammer."

"Thank you, Samuel." Darren obviously knew the man. "Samuel Winterman, Violet Rhinehammer."

Though Holiday Junction was small, I still didn't know everyone who lived here.

Mr. Winterman slightly bowed, and I curtsied with a laugh to play along.

I could almost hear Mama's voice in my head, her Southern drawl rich with excitement. *"That place is booked solid for the next year, Violet! You just wait and see! Every well-to-do family is fighting to spend their holidays there. It's the talk of the town, I tell you. You should do a write-up about it."*

And knowing Mama, there was probably a kernel of truth to her proclamation. But booked for a whole year? That still seemed like a stretch.

I looked up at Darren, my heart full. "This is beautiful," I said. "But I think we are underdressed."

"Nonsense," Darren said with a smile.

Samuel swung open the door, which obliged with a soft creak, and the warmth from inside hit us like a wave. The lobby was even more extravagant than I could have imagined. A massive stone fireplace dominated the room, its flames crackling merrily as stockings embroidered with gold thread, each one as large as a person, hung from the mantel. Garland wrapped every banister and beam, adorned with lights, pinecones, and velvet bows. The scents of fresh pine, cinnamon, and gingerbread filled the air, enveloping me in a sense of Christmas.

In the center of the room stood another towering Christmas tree, its branches heavy with ornaments in every color imaginable. Glass chandeliers hung from the vaulted ceiling, casting soft light that danced across the polished wood floors, and everywhere I looked, guests were laughing, sipping mulled wine, and marveling at the surrounding beauty.

Darren led me farther inside, his hand resting lightly on the small of my back as we took in the atmosphere. "So," he said with a grin, "what do you think?"

I turned to him, still amazed by the sheer scale of it all. "I think... this might just be the most beautiful place I've ever seen." I blinked a few times, still trying to take in the scene.

Before Darren could respond, I heard a familiar voice followed by the click of heels on the hard floor.

"There y'all are."

I turned just in time to see my mama, Millie Kay, sweeping into the room like a queen holding court.

She was decked out in an emerald-green velvet

gown that skimmed the floor, well fitted to her curves, with a strand of pearls that lay elegantly along her collarbone. Her hair, as always, was styled to perfection, not a single strand out of place.

"Well, there's my girl," she called out, her Southern drawl dripping with excitement. She opened her arms wide, as if the room itself was her doing. "Can you believe it, Violet? Isn't it grand?"

"Mama, what are you doing here?" I asked, still trying to process everything. My eyes slid down to a name tag with her name and an etched outline of the lodge.

Then I noticed my daddy step out from behind the massive stone counter at the far side of the room, looking just as dapper as ever, with a top hat perched jauntily on his head and a twinkle in his eye. He wasn't exactly the sort to wear a top hat, and I narrowed my eyes at him, suspicion rising. He too wore a name tag.

"Mama?" I asked slowly, looking between her and Daddy, who was now grinning like the cat that got the cream. "What's going on here?"

Mama gave me a once-over, her eyebrows lifting as she took in my coat and snow boots. "Violet, sweetie, it's the grand opening. You could've worn something nicer." She pointed her perfectly manicured finger toward my boyfriend. "I mean, just look at Darren."

I whipped around to face him, and my mouth dropped open at the sight of him in a sleek black tuxedo. "What the... When did you?" I had been too distracted to notice the change in Darren's attire when he'd slipped out of his heavy coat.

Darren grinned sheepishly, shrugging one shoulder. "Surprise?"

I looked between the tuxedo-clad Darren and my parents, my mind scrambling to catch up with everything happening. "What is going on here?" I asked again, feeling like I was missing a very important piece of information.

Daddy walked over and rested his hand on the counter as though it were his personal domain. "Well now, Violet, you know I like to help out whenever I can. I've been bored sitting around the house." He tipped his top hat in a playful gesture. "Your mama and I just figured we'd pitch in for the grand opening. It's a big night, after all."

I narrowed my eyes further. "Since when do you wear a top hat to 'help out,' Daddy?"

Darren's laughter was soft and full of tenderness as he stepped closer, taking both of my hands in his. "Violet," he said, his voice gentle, "there's something you should know. I've been working on this project for a while."

I tilted my head, utterly confused. "What project?" I asked.

"The lodge," he said, smiling that mischievous smile of his that always meant he was up to something. "I bought it."

I blinked. Once. Twice. "You... bought the lodge?" I spit out the question.

"I've been fixing it up for the past year." Darren nodded, his eyes bright with amusement.

I opened my mouth then closed it again, at a complete loss for words. How had I not known about this? How had he managed to keep such a massive project a secret?

"Bought it *and* restored it," Mama added, giving Darren an approving nod. "You should've seen this place before he got his hands on it, Violet. It was falling apart. Roof leaking, windows broken. But look at it now. It's the talk of the town, and not just in *my* circles." She winked, clearly proud of Darren's work. "I wasn't exaggerating when I said it was booked solid. Everyone wants a piece of the new Christmas Lodge."

Darren squeezed my hands, his gaze softening as he watched my reaction. "I wanted it to be a surprise," he explained gently. "Something special for you... and for the town. I know how you love hearing all the tales about how much I loved Christmas as a child, how magical it was. I thought maybe we could bring that magic back."

My heart swelled, and for a moment, all the noise

of the grand room faded. It was just me, standing in front of the man who had brought back a piece of Holiday Junction's history, not for himself, but for me.

"You did all this?" I whispered, my voice catching in my throat.

Darren smiled and pulled me into a soft hug, his chin resting on the top of my head. "For the town. And I want you to be part of it."

Tears pricked the corners of my eyes, but I blinked them away quickly, unwilling to cry in the middle of this grand celebration. "I can't believe it," I said, my voice barely above a whisper. "This is... this is amazing, Darren."

"Now, now," Mama said, her voice full of good-natured impatience. "No more standing around. Violet, you need to go change into something proper for the grand opening. We have appearances to make."

I pulled back from Darren's embrace, still feeling a little dazed but full of gratitude. "What am I even supposed to wear to something like this? I didn't exactly bring a ball gown."

"Don't worry, sweetie. I've got just the thing upstairs. We've planned for this." Mama waved her hand dismissively.

I stared at her, my mouth hanging open again. "*You* planned for this?" The questions just kept coming.

"Of course I did," Millie Kay said with a sly smile. "You think I'd let you come to the grand opening of the lodge looking anything less than fabulous?"

I shot Darren an incredulous look, but he just grinned and shrugged, as if to say, *What can you do?*

"Mama, what are you talking about?" I asked, following her as she led me toward the grand staircase.

The staircase was something straight out of a fairytale. The steps swept upward in a graceful curve, with polished wooden banisters wrapped in garland and twinkling lights, each step leading higher into the grand, glowing lodge. The warmth from the giant stone fireplace below sent flickers of light dancing along the walls, and as we reached the landing, I glanced back down at the lobby.

The view from above was stunning. The oversized Christmas tree shone in the center of the room, and below, guests mingled, the sounds of laughter and holiday cheer echoing softly. I paused for a moment to take in the joy, my breath catching as the full scope of what Darren had accomplished washed over me.

Mama didn't slow down, though. She turned to me, her face glowing with excitement. "Violet, I'm surprised you hadn't figured this out already. Darren's been planning this project for ages. You know, his parents took him up here for so many years."

I blinked, taking in her words. Of course, I knew

some things about Darren's childhood, and he'd mentioned the lodge, but he'd never once expressed a desire to reopen it.

Mama led me to one of the suites. When she opened the door, I gasped. It was like walking into a royal chamber. The room was decorated to the nines —plush velvet furniture, gold-framed mirrors, and garlands wrapped around every doorframe and window. The scents of pine and cinnamon filled the air, and the light from the chandelier above sparkled like diamonds on the ceiling.

And there, hanging on a mannequin near the enormous four-poster bed, was a dress. Not just any dress—a gorgeous, flowing gown that shimmered in the soft light. The material was a deep sapphire blue, perfect for the season, and I knew instantly the color would complement my long blond hair.

Mama beamed as she walked over to the dress and ran her fingers over the fabric. "You'll look just stunning in this," she said, her Southern drawl sweet and proud. "It's the grand opening, after all. Darren wanted everything to be perfect for you."

I felt a lump rising in my throat as I stepped toward the dress. "Mama, this is all so... overwhelming."

"Nonsense," Mama said, waving her hand as she busied herself with straightening the dress. "It's a dream come true, is what it is. You slip into this dress, and you'll feel like the belle of the ball."

I started to change, slipping out of my coat and boots. As I pulled the dress on, the fabric hugged me in all the right places, flowing gracefully to the floor.

Mama kept talking as I dressed, her voice full of affection. "You know, Darren's been working on this for so long. He's poured his heart into this place. He wanted everything to be just right for when he finally shared it with you. And now, look at you. You're part of it, just like he always wanted."

Before I could respond, a soft knock sounded at the door.

"Come in," Mama called, her voice still chipper.

The door opened, and Darren stepped in. He was looking down at something in his hand, but when he glanced up and saw me standing there in the gown, his mouth fell open.

He blinked, as though trying to find the right words, but all that came out was a soft "Wow."

My cheeks warmed under his gaze. "Do I look okay?" I asked, smoothing my hands nervously over the dress.

Darren shook his head slowly, his dark eyes never leaving mine. "You look... breathtaking."

We just stared at each other, the space between us heavy with emotion.

But then Mama, ever one to keep things moving, interrupted the moment. "Well, Darren, are they here?" she asked, her eyes bright with excitement.

Darren tore his gaze from me. "Uh, yes," he said, his voice still a little hoarse. He nodded slowly. "They're here."

"Who's here?" I asked, looking between them both, confused yet again.

Mama's smile widened, her eyes full of mischief. "*Southern Charm* magazine," she said proudly, her voice dripping with excitement. "They're doing a feature on the lodge and the grand opening."

My eyes widened as the news sank in. "*Southern Charm?*" I repeated, feeling a rush of nervous energy. That was one of the biggest lifestyle magazines in the South.

"Yes, sweetie," Mama said, practically bouncing with excitement. "They're going to showcase everything—Darren's restoration work, the grand opening, and, of course, you and him as the stars of the story. Isn't it just the most exciting thing?"

I looked over at Darren, who was still standing there, his gaze full of adoration.

"I thought you deserved to be part of this," he said quietly, "and now you will be."

"It's time someone does some good reporting on you and not the other way around," Mama said, practically shoving us out the suite's door. "Now, go on and smile. Like you were taught in all of them classes when you were young."

Darren took my hand, and together we started

down the grand staircase. The moment we stepped onto the landing, the crowd went silent. The murmur of voices and the clinking of glasses hushed as all eyes turned toward us. The glow of the chandelier cast a subtle radiance on the gathered guests, while the massive Christmas tree glittered in the background, its ornaments reflecting the energy of the evening.

At the base of the stairs, a server balanced a silver tray with two tall flutes of champagne. Darren squeezed my hand gently before releasing it and stepping forward to take one of the glasses. He handed it to me with a small smile, then picked up the second glass for himself.

I could feel the weight of the crowd's gaze on us. From the corner of my eye, I spotted the photographers from *Southern Charm* magazine, their cameras flashing as they attempted to capture every detail. My heart raced with a mixture of nerves and excitement. This wasn't the kind of attention I was used to—I was usually behind the scenes, writing about other people's stories, not the focus of one.

Darren turned toward me, his dark eyes warm and full of pride. "To the grand reopening of the Christmas Lodge," he began, his voice carrying across the room. The champagne flute in his hand gleamed under the light as he raised it high. "This year marks the beginning of something truly special for Holiday

Junction. It's a celebration of tradition, community, and the magic of the holiday season."

The crowd watched in rapt attention, and I couldn't help but feel the weight of the moment. Darren's voice was strong and confident, making him the perfect host for such a grand occasion.

"With the reopening of the lodge," he continued, his voice filled with excitement, "we're also kicking off this year's month-long Christmas Market, where we will celebrate the best of what Holiday Junction has to offer."

I smiled up at him, feeling the warmth of his words spread through me. But then Darren paused, his eyes sparkling with something deeper—something I couldn't quite place.

"And," he said, his voice softening as he looked directly at me, "to make this year even more special, I'm honored to announce that we're moving the Mistletoe Masquerade Ball to the Christmas Lodge to mark the official end of the festival."

There was a murmur of excitement from the crowd, but before I could fully absorb what he'd said, Darren added, "And I have it on good authority from the Merry Maker himself that this is just the beginning of the surprises in store for Holiday Junction this year."

The words hit me like a snowball to the chest.

My smile faltered, and I turned to look at Darren,

my eyes wide in disbelief. *The Merry Maker?* How could he have just casually announced something about the Merry Maker—especially since we were the Merry Makers, and that was a *huge* secret?

Before I could say anything, a spotlight shifted, illuminating the far side of the room where the grand ballroom doors stood closed. The crowd turned to look as the massive double doors slowly swung open to reveal the ballroom beyond. But that wasn't the only thing catching people's attention.

In the center of the ballroom stood a large cutout replica of the lodge, beautifully detailed down to the tiniest window and wreath. But it wasn't just any decoration. It was the Merry Maker's signature mark —the symbol that had come to represent the final event of the month-long festival. And Darren had just made it the centerpiece of the grand reopening.

I stared at the scene in shock, barely able to process what I was seeing. Darren had made a decision—our decision—without even telling me.

The crowd erupted in applause, completely unaware of the storm brewing inside me. Darren turned to face me, his face beaming with pride, but I couldn't force myself to return his smile. My heart pounded in my chest as I tried to wrap my head around what had just happened.

How could he have done this? The Merry Maker was a secret—a tradition that had been passed down through generations. Darren and I had taken on the role together, working to bring a little extra magic to the town every Christmas. But this? This was a public announcement that put our secret work right in the spotlight.

"Darren," I whispered, my voice tight with emotion, "what... what have you done?"

He looked at me, the joy in his eyes fading as he realized something was wrong. "Violet," he began, his voice low and full of concern, "I thought this would make everything even more special. I wanted to surprise you."

"A surprise?" I repeated, shaking my head slightly, my voice barely above a whisper. "The Merry Maker is supposed to be a *secret*, Darren. This wasn't your decision to make alone."

His face fell, and for a moment, he looked as though he'd been stricken. "I didn't mean to overstep," he said softly, his hand reaching for mine. "I just thought... I thought this would be perfect. For us. For the lodge. For the town."

Darren had always been thoughtful, always included me in decisions that mattered, especially when it came to the Merry Maker. But this time, he'd taken matters into his own hands, and the weight of that decision felt heavy.

Before I could say anything more, Mama, oblivious to the tension between us, leaned in with a delighted grin. "Well now, isn't this just wonderful? The Merry Maker's mark on the lodge for all to see. *Southern Charm* will eat this up."

I finally forced a smile, the corners of my lips tight. "Yes, Mama. Wonderful."

CHAPTER THREE

"I can't believe you did all of this," I said, letting the whole Merry Maker thing slide for now.

I tried to be grateful that he'd taken one more thing off my plate. Most of the time, getting Darren to help with the Merry Maker decisions was like pulling teeth, especially when it came to where the Merry Maker sign would go.

"It's taken a while, but I sure hope Holiday Junction benefits from it," Darren said, draping his arm around me as we walked deeper into the lodge. His warmth and steady presence settled me as we moved toward the grand ballroom, where the indoor market was in full swing.

When we stepped inside, the view took my breath away. Darren had taken what was once a formal ballroom and turned it into a holiday haven. The high ceilings were strung with garlands of pine, holly, and lights, giving the space an enchanted look. The air was rich with the scents of cinnamon, fresh pine, and something sweet—likely from the roasted chestnuts and warm gingerbread being served at the Sugarbrush Bakery booth.

All around the room, local vendors had set up booths, each one overflowing with Christmas-themed goods. Wooden tables were laden with handmade crafts, from delicate wreaths wrapped in ribbon to Vern McKenna's hand-carved wooden figurines of snowmen, reindeer, and jolly Santas. Glittering ornaments dangled from tree branches strung along the booths, their bright colors reflecting the warm glow of the lights above. There were hand-knit scarves and mittens, jars of homemade preserves, and even steaming mugs of hot chocolate lined up from the Brewing Beans booth near the center.

"There he is," Darren said softly, pointing ahead. "Lionel's toy shop was closed for years, and it's great to see him back, making this year's ornament."

I smiled, watching Lionel work. The man had a kind, grandfatherly look about him, his silver hair peeking out from beneath a green velvet cap, his hands steady despite his age. His workbench was surrounded by some of his finest creations, rare and priceless ornaments from years gone by. These weren't for sale, merely on display for the town's residents to admire.

"This is incredible," I murmured, my eyes sweeping over the delicate decorations.

Each one was a work of art in its own right. The small replicas depicted the town's iconic landmarks, like the fountain in Celebration Park, the Christmas Lodge itself, and even the old candy shop. These rare pieces were a nod to Holiday Junction's rich history, their craftsmanship a reminder of the charm that had always been a part of the town.

"These are amazing." I was in awe of all of Lionel's work.

"Thank you." Lionel smiled but didn't look up.

He was working on this year's ornament, a miniature hand-painted replica of the newly restored Christmas Lodge. The workmanship was stunning. The tiny lodge shimmered with golden lights, a dusting of snow on its roof and a miniature wreath adorning the front door. Even the large icicles hanging from the eaves seemed lifelike. Every detail, from the glowing windows to the tiny snow-covered trees lining the path, had been carefully painted by Lionel himself.

"Mr. Garland, I'd like to introduce you to Violet Rhinehammer," Darren said.

Lionel looked up from his work then, taking

more of a vested interest in me than before, his blue eyes peering from behind his round glasses. "Well, it's a pleasure to meet you, Miss Rhinehammer," he said, giving me a gentle smile. "I've heard a lot about you."

"Your work is... breathtaking." I returned his smile.

"Thank you, my dear," he said, his voice gravelly but kind. "It's been an honor to make the ornament again after all these years."

As we spoke, a group from *Southern Charm* magazine hovered nearby, their cameras snapping away. They focused on Lionel's work, capturing the delicate process of painting the ornament and documenting the entire scene. Flashes went off as the photographers took shots of the rare ornaments from previous years that were arranged neatly on a red velvet cloth for the public to admire.

I watched the scene unfold, feeling a pang of envy. "It's too bad I wasn't able to capture all of this for the *Junction Journal*," I said quietly to Darren.

The truth was, I had spent years searching for that big scoop, the one that would make my career go viral. But now, things were different. I still wanted my stories to reach people, but my focus had shifted. I wanted to bring more light to Holiday Junction, to show the world how unique this town really was.

"Actually, you'll be able to do just that," Darren

said. "Radley and your mama have been working on it behind the scenes."

"What?" I asked, surprised.

He grinned. "Radley's been taking photos all evening, and your mama's been making sure everything's documented. They've been quietly putting together a whole spread for you to feature in the *Junction Journal*. It'll be one of your best stories yet," he said.

I blinked, the surprise washing over me. "Darren... I don't know what to say." I was shocked. He'd thought of everything.

"You don't have to say anything. You've worked hard for Holiday Junction. You've brought so much tourism back to the village over the last couple of years, and you deserve this." He gave my hand a gentle squeeze.

I smiled up at him, my heart full.

Maybe I hadn't captured the story myself, but thanks to Darren—and with a little help from my family and friends—I'd still be able to tell the tale of the Christmas Lodge's grand reopening, an event that brought the heart of the town to light.

As the *Southern Charm* photographers continued snapping photos, I knew one thing for sure. This was going to be a Christmas I'd never forget.

"Want to go walk around a little more?" Darren asked.

"Yes. Of course I do," I said with so much excitement. "Even though you've covered all the prework for the article, I still want to see everything through my own eyes."

We continued to walk through the holiday market inside the ballroom. The sounds of laughter, jingling bells, and festive music filled the air. I was overjoyed to see Emily's daughter, Katie, playing a festive tune on the piano.

"Hey." I tapped Darren on the chest playfully. "Where are the Mad Fiddlers?"

"Don't you worry." Darren wiggled his brows. "We will be up there before the month is over."

"That's ridiculous," a woman muttered as she passed, knocking into my shoulder without bothering to apologize. "Same designs year after year." She threw her hands up in the air.

"That's Evelyn Frost," Darren said quietly, leaning in so I could hear him over the chatter. "She was in the running for the ornament design this year but lost out to Mr. Garland. She's not exactly thrilled about it."

That caught my attention.

While I appeared to be looking at the wreath booth, I observed Evelyn carefully. Evelyn Frost was all sleek lines and sharp edges, her black hair styled in a tight bun.

"Evelyn, nice to see you," Darren said politely.

Her lips twitched into what might have been a smile when she glanced up at Darren.

She stood rigid, arms crossed tightly over her chest, fingers gripping her elbows, all hinting at deeper frustration.

Evelyn's smile widened, though it didn't reach her eyes. "Darren," she purred, her voice smooth as silk. "What a magical evening, isn't it?" She glanced at me then, her eyes flicking up and down in a subtle assessment. "And you must be Violet Rhinehammer," she said, her tone light but tinged with something I couldn't quite place. "I've heard so much about you."

"All good, I hope," I replied with a polite smile, though something about the way she said my name put me on edge.

"Of course," Evelyn said smoothly, but her gaze quickly shifted back to Lionel, who was engrossed in his work. "Such a beautiful tradition, the annual ornament. I was so looking forward to being a part of it this year. Well, the council had other ideas." Her voice was pleasant, but her knuckles had turned white from gripping her elbows too tightly. "Since you are a journalist, I think you need to look into this as an investigation."

Before I could respond, Darren cleared his throat.

"We should probably let Evelyn go." Darren pointed to her booth. "She's got customers."

"And now that *Southern Charm* is here for him"—

she threw a look to Lionel—"I've got to get some new custom jobs." She continued, "Of course, Lionel is very talented… especially for someone who's been out of the game for so long."

I caught the edge in her words, but Darren was already steering me away from the booth, his arm tightening around my shoulders as we moved through the crowd.

"She's just bitter about the competition," he whispered to me.

"She's really mad," I replied. Something about Evelyn Frost lingered in the back of my mind.

We were weaving through the market when Darren suddenly stopped in his tracks. I followed his gaze to a man standing near one of the vendors, casually inspecting a hand-carved wooden reindeer.

"Gregory?" Darren said, his voice full of surprise.

The man turned, and when he saw Darren, a smile spread across his face, though it didn't quite reach his pale-blue eyes. His lean figure seemed almost out of place among the festive crowd—his clothes were simple, but his posture was stiff, as though he wasn't entirely comfortable in his own skin.

"Darren," the man said, nodding. "Long time no see."

Darren quickly recovered from his initial shock and turned to me. "Violet, this is Gregory Garland.

Lionel's younger brother. Gregory, this is my friend, Violet Rhinehammer."

Friend?

It took everything in me to plant a smile on my face.

Gregory extended his hand to me, and as I shook it, I noticed how cold and firm his grip was. His eyes met mine briefly, but they flicked away almost immediately, as though he was avoiding something.

"Nice to meet you," he said, his voice smooth but distant.

"Likewise," I replied, sensing the tension in the air.

"I didn't know you were back in town," Darren said, his tone casual but laced with curiosity. "How long have you been here?"

"Just moved back recently," Gregory said with a dismissive wave of his hand, his lips curling into a tight smile. "Needed a change of scenery, I guess."

"After all these years? I thought you were settled elsewhere." Darren didn't let the vague answer go.

Gregory shrugged, his eyes scanning the room as though he were looking for an escape. "Things change," he said cryptically before glancing over at Lionel's booth. His gaze lingered on his older brother for a moment longer than necessary, his mouth twitching slightly before he quickly masked it with another tight smile. "It's good to be back, though. Holiday Junction hasn't changed much, has it?"

Darren seemed ready to press further, but I caught his arm gently, giving him a small shake of my head. Something about Gregory's demeanor—his shifty eyes, the way he avoided looking directly at Darren—told me he wasn't ready to reveal much, at least not yet.

"Well," Darren said, recovering smoothly, "it's good to have you back. Maybe we can catch up later at the bar. Drinks on me."

Darren was not only a lawyer, and not only now the owner of the Christmas Lodge, but he was also the owner of a dive bar that didn't really have a name. I called it the Jiggle Joint—you know, the kind of place that has a stage for some jiggling. It was rare, though, to see jiggling the likes for which the stage had been intended when the first owner had opened the place.

"Sure," Gregory said, though his smile didn't seem sincere. "Later."

With brows furrowed in concern, Darren watched him go. "I haven't seen Gregory in years," Darren murmured, almost to himself. "He left town without saying much to anyone."

"Do you think he's here for Lionel?" I asked and glanced up at Darren.

Darren hesitated then shook his head. "I don't know. He's always been distant." Darren shrugged it off. "I'll see what he says at the bar when he stops by."

"And how do you know he'll stop by?" I questioned Darren's assured demeanor.

"I've never seen Gregory turn down a free drink." Darren snickered as we continued our walk through the amazing opening of the lodge and the indoor Christmas market.

CHAPTER FOUR

Back in my apartment, I kicked my boots off by the door and shrugged out of my coat before hanging it on the hook. I'd changed back into my warm clothes before Darren and I left the lodge.

Only, we hadn't left in the fun sleigh. Since it was late, the horses had been taken back to their barn at the Hippity Hop Farm, and the coachman was likely tucked snugly in his bed.

Here I was, back home, reminiscing about everything that had happened earlier and almost questioning whether it had been real.

The warmth of the evening lingered, filling me with a buzzing excitement. It had been such a lovely night with the market, the twinkling lights, the festive booths filled with holiday treasures. Darren had gone above and beyond, and even now, I couldn't believe he'd organized everything so seamlessly.

My parents had been there, looking proud, and the reporters from *Southern Charm* magazine had been snapping photos of Lionel's incredible ornaments. It all felt like something from a dream. And yet, here I was, too wired to sleep, thoughts of the grand reopening of the Christmas Lodge still swirling in my mind.

I paced around the living room for a moment, the memories of the night replaying in my mind—the way Darren had surprised me with the secret of Mama and Radley collecting all the information so I could draft an amazing article for the *Junction Journal*, the knowing look in his eye when he caught me staring at the glowing ornaments Lionel had crafted. Everything had been so romantic, so perfect.

Unable to sleep, I made my way to my small desk that sat in front of the window near the balcony. The desk was tucked into the corner of my living room, a cozy little nook with a view of downtown Holiday Junction's art district. From my seat, I could see the cobblestone street below, winding like a frozen river through the heart of the town. Farther down the mountain, I could see downtown Holiday Junction and Celebration Park.

I opened my laptop, the soft glow of the screen lighting up the room as I tried to organize my thoughts for the article I planned to write. But as much as I wanted to focus, the scene outside was too beautiful to ignore. I found myself looking out the window, letting the serenity of the art district at night wash over me.

The street below was bathed in a faint yellow light, and the old-fashioned carriage lamps that lined the sidewalks sent shimmering shadows across the cobblestones, making the snow shine as if someone had scattered a million tiny diamonds.

Icicles hung from the eaves of the buildings, long and sharp, catching the lamplight and refracting it in every direction. The icicles pointed toward the ground like icy daggers, a clear sign that the temperature had dropped well below freezing. But there was something so magical about it all—the cold, the quiet, the way the snow seemed to muffle the sounds of the town, creating a peaceful stillness.

My breath fogged up the glass as I leaned closer, watching the flakes of snow swirl and dance in the light. It was nearly midnight, and the streets were mostly deserted, save for the occasional couple walking hand in hand, their boots crunching in the snow. Lights in the display windows of a few art galleries and cafés spilled out into the night. The town felt frozen in time, a winter wonderland preserved in the hush of the late hour.

I smiled to myself, thinking about how lucky I

was to live here, in a place where the magic of the holidays never seemed to fade, no matter how cold the winter nights grew.

Even a deep freeze couldn't take away the warmth that seemed to radiate from the town's heart.

From my window, the distant lights of the outdoor Christmas Market looked like a halo over the lodge. It was just a glimmer from here, but I knew it would soon be the talk of the town, especially with *Southern Charm* magazine covering the event. The thought sent a spark of excitement through me.

This was it, the moment Holiday Junction would shine, and I would be part of telling its story.

I glanced back at my laptop, the cursor blinking impatiently on the empty page. Inspiration buzzed through my veins, but my thoughts were too scattered to put into words. I stared out at the snow-covered streets again, letting my mind drift.

Shivering slightly, I pulled my blanket tighter around my shoulders.

I just couldn't go to sleep, so I decided to type out what I had seen.

It almost seemed as though the blank page taunted me. The words were there, bubbling up inside, but they hadn't quite arranged themselves in the right order. My fingers hovered over the keys, and I felt the familiar anticipation of starting a new story—

the thrill of capturing a moment that would, hopefully, inspire others the way it had inspired me.

With a deep breath, I started to type.

The soft click-clack of the keys filled the quiet of the room, blending with the distant hum of the radiator warming the space. Each tap felt like an exhilarating spark as the night's events began to spill out onto the screen. I could practically feel the texture of the evening coming back to me—the glittering lights, the scents of cinnamon and pine, the laughter that had filled the market. The words flowed easily now, fueled by my love for Holiday Junction.

"Tonight, the Christmas Lodge was more than just a building reopening its doors," I typed, my fingers dancing across the keyboard. "It was a revival of everything this town stands for—community, tradition, and the magic that has always made Holiday Junction so special."

I paused for a moment, staring out the window again. The snow was falling softly now, each flake catching the light and swirling before settling on the cobblestones. The streets were still deserted—peaceful and untouched. There was something almost surreal about how quiet it was, as if the town was holding its breath, waiting for something to happen.

My thoughts drifted back to Darren, to the way

he had looked at me when we'd stood in the market, watching Lionel craft the ornament. That twinkle in his eye, the warmth of his hand in mine... those had been such precious moments. And then, of course, my parents had been there, sharing in the joy. It was as though everything I had worked toward, everything I had wanted for Holiday Junction, had finally come together.

But even in the perfection of the night, there had been small, sharp moments—Evelyn's cold dismissal, Gregory's distant smile. I shook my head, trying to push those thoughts away for now. Tonight wasn't the night for digging into the mysteries behind their unease. Tonight was about capturing the magic.

I began typing again, letting my fingers fly over the keys.

"As the snow fell and the twinkling lights illuminated the Christmas Market, it felt like stepping into a storybook, one where the past, present, and future of Holiday Junction were intertwined in the most magical way." I spoke the lines to myself as I typed.

The words came faster now, each one filled with the excitement that had been buzzing in me since the moment I had arrived at the lodge. Even though Radley had been taking photos throughout the evening, I wanted my own snapshots, my own memories. Something about holding the camera, framing the shots myself, helped me feel more connected to the story I was telling.

I paused again, staring at the paragraph I'd just written. The blinking cursor seemed to be urging me to continue, but my mind was already elsewhere. I couldn't stop thinking about the lodge, the way it had glowed from a distance, the warmth that had radiated from every corner. The place was beautiful, yes, but there was something more to it than that. Something deeper.

With a small sigh, I hit Save on my document and closed the laptop. I wasn't going to finish the article tonight—there was too much energy in me, too many thoughts racing around in my mind that I couldn't pin down just yet.

As I gazed out the window again, my eyes traced the familiar outline of the lodge in the distance. The glow of the Christmas Market was faint but still there, like a beacon on Darren's lighthouse calling me back. I knew the market had probably closed for the night, and most people had already gone home, but that didn't stop the pull I felt toward the lodge. I wanted to see it again through my own lens.

After making up my mind, I stood and grabbed my camera from the shelf by the door. My fingers brushed the cold metal, and a spark of anticipation ran through me. I slipped my boots back on, pulled my warm coat tight around me, wrapped my scarf snugly around my neck, and tucked my hair into a stocking hat.

A fresh rush of cold air hit me as I stepped out onto the balcony for a moment to peer down once more at the snow-covered streets below.

The icicles hanging from the edge of the roof were longer than they had been earlier, the sharp points glistening in the streetlights.

The chill told me the temperature had dropped even further, but I didn't mind. I was too excited, too driven by the need to capture the beauty of the night on my own terms.

With my camera slung over my shoulder and new energy in my step, I made my way down the stairs and out the front door. The cold nipped at my cheeks as I stepped out onto the quiet street, and the silence added to the ambience. The snow crunched beneath my boots as I walked toward the lodge.

When I reached the edge of the Christmas Lodge property, I felt as though I was seeing the place for the first time. It was gorgeous, like a scene straight out of a holiday movie. I lifted my camera, framed the lodge in the center of the shot, and snapped a few photos, the shutter clicking softly in the stillness of the night.

There was no one around, no movement except for the gently falling snow. It was just me, my camera, and the quiet magic of the town. I walked closer to the lodge and took a few more photos of the lights, the snow-covered trees, and the rows of market booths that stood empty now, waiting for the next day's festivities. Even the icicles hanging around the lodge's windows made for a gorgeous photo. The scene brought to mind one of those snow-globe villages I'd seen at the Holiday Market. Timeless, peaceful, and still.

It was peaceful, and yet, there was a strange feeling creeping up the back of my neck. A sense that I wasn't quite alone. I stopped for a moment, scanning the quiet street, but there was nothing out of place. The town was asleep, and I was just a woman with her camera, trying to capture the magic of the night.

The heavy wooden door, adorned with a lush evergreen wreath and twinkling lights, creaked softly as I pushed it open. A rush of warmth greeted me, along with the familiar scents of pine and cinnamon, instantly cocooning me in the festive comfort of the Christmas Lodge.

Inside, the lodge was even quieter than the streets. The lights strung along the rafters reflected off the glossy wooden floors, and a crackling fire in the grand stone fireplace flickered near the other end of the room. The sounds of my footsteps were muffled by a thick rug beneath me.

The front counter stood just ahead, and its polished surface reflected the light of the chandeliers hanging above. The light was on, but no one stood there to greet me.

I paused for a moment, glancing around. It was well past midnight, and anyone staying at the lodge had probably long since tucked themselves into bed and were now snuggled under blankets with visions of sugarplums dancing in their heads.

A faint sound caught my ear, and I turned toward the source. It was the familiar jingle of a Christmas movie theme, the kind that played nonstop during the holiday season. The sound was coming from somewhere behind the counter, and I couldn't help but smile as I realized what was happening.

The employee on duty was likely nestled away in a back room, enjoying a late-night holiday-movie marathon while the guests slept. I imagined them curled up in a chair, sipping hot cocoa, wrapped in a warm blanket and totally unaware that I'd slipped inside the lodge.

The temptation to call out was there, to let them know I was around, but something about the quiet, the magic of being in this place alone, made me hesitate. Besides, I wasn't planning to stay long, just long enough to take a few more photos of the lodge in its nighttime glory.

I turned away from the counter, letting my feet

guide me deeper into the lobby. The Christmas tree in the center of the room still twinkled brightly, its ornaments shimmering in the firelight. I pulled my camera from my shoulder and adjusted the settings to capture the perfect shot. The soft *click* of the shutter echoed in the quiet room as I snapped photos of the tree, the fireplace, the wreaths hanging from the walls.

Every corner of the lodge was wrapped in holiday warmth, and for a moment, I felt like I was in my own little Christmas world.

I wandered through the space, the soft hum of the movie from behind the counter blending into the background as I moved toward the grand staircase. Outside, icicles clung to the large window panes, and the snow continued to fall in soft, lazy drifts. I framed a shot through the window at the far end of the room, capturing the snow-covered market booths that were bathed in the light from the lodge.

As I lowered my camera, a soft creak made me pause. I glanced toward the staircase, where the wooden railing curved up to the second floor, the banister wrapped in garlands and lights. There was no one there—at least, no one I could see.

But something felt off. I couldn't place it, but the feeling crept up the back of my neck, raising goosebumps on my arms despite the warmth of the room.

I shook my head, chalking the apprehension up to

being overtired and hopped-up about the holidays. After all, I had been buzzing with energy all night, and it was well past the time I should've been asleep.

With a deep breath, I turned back toward the front desk, eager to get one last shot of the tree before heading home. But just as I raised my camera, the creak came again, this time louder, echoing through the empty lodge.

I froze and glanced around the room once more. The lodge was still empty, as far as I could tell, but the faint echo of the creak hung in the air. The sound had been too loud to be the settling of the old wood. *Someone was up there.*

For a moment, I considered calling out to ask if anyone else was awake.

Trying to let go of the uneasy feeling that had crept over me, I shook my head and reminded myself I was likely just overthinking things. Who was I to question someone else's late-night wanderings? Maybe they, like me, were too wired from the evening's excitement to sleep.

I headed toward the ballroom, where the indoor holiday market had been set up earlier that evening. I could still picture the event—the warm smiles of the vendors and the beautiful array of handcrafted goods. The memory of it made me feel a little more grounded, the sense of unease starting to melt away.

The ballroom was quiet now, the festive energy of

the market replaced with a peaceful stillness. But even in the quiet, the booths were still brimming with holiday cheer—wreaths hanging, sparkling ornaments dangling from tree branches, and small displays of toys and decorations carefully arranged.

I held up my camera, framing a shot of the booths, the lights reflecting off the ornaments in a way that made them look like tiny stars scattered throughout the room. The soft *click* of the shutter echoed gently as I captured the beauty of the market at night, each photo more stunning than the last.

The dim lighting added a touch of mystery to the scene, casting soft shadows across the displays. I slowly moved through the room, snapping photos as I went. My excitement grew with each shot, the article starting to take shape in my mind. I knew it would come together with just the right balance of charm, history, and warm holiday spirit.

Finally, I reached the booth where Lionel Garland had proudly displayed his antique ornaments. The rare, handcrafted pieces were truly collector's items. The elegant models reflected the long heritage of the town, each one labeled with its respective year. I crouched down slightly and adjusted the focus on my camera to capture the details of each ornament. The shimmer of the lights around me added a sweet glow to the fragile pieces.

Through the eye piece, something seemed weird. Off.

I lowered the camera, my brow furrowing as I looked more closely at the booth. I squinted, noticing that a few of the ornaments had fallen off their stands, pieces lying broken on the floor and glittering shards scattered across the booth.

I took a cautious step forward, my heart beginning to race. *Why didn't I notice this before?*

And then I saw it.

Behind the booth, crumpled in a heap, was Mr. Lionel Garland.

For a moment, I froze, my brain struggling to comprehend what my eyes were seeing. His silver hair that had been neatly combed was disheveled, and the green velvet cap he'd been wearing earlier lay on the floor beside him, half-hidden by the shattered remains of his antique ornaments. His body lay unnaturally still, surrounded by broken toys and decorations, their once beautiful craftsmanship now destroyed in a chaotic mess.

My breath caught in my throat as I stared, unable to move, unable to process the scene in front of me.

"Mr. Garland?" I whispered, my voice shaky and small in the vast silence of the ballroom.

There was no response.

I took a hesitant step forward, my eyes locked on

his still form. He looked peaceful, almost as though he had simply fallen asleep at his booth, but the scattered, broken pieces around him told a different story. My gaze moved to his face. His eyes were closed, his mouth slightly parted, and his skin had a pale, waxy sheen that made my stomach twist with dread.

"Mr. Garland?" I tried again, louder this time. Still no answer.

A cold chill ran down my spine, the weight of the situation starting to sink in. I hurried around the booth, careful not to step on the broken ornaments. My mind raced as I knelt beside him, searching for any sign of life, any indication that he might still have been breathing. But when I touched his wrist to find a pulse, the truth hit me like the crash of a falling icicle.

Sudden, cold, and impossible to ignore.

He was gone.

My heart pounded in my chest as I stood up, stumbling back slightly. His body was still warm, but the lifelessness was unmistakable. There were no visible signs of injury—no blood, no wounds—just the eerie stillness of a man who had been full of life only hours earlier.

For a moment, I wondered if it had been a heart attack. He'd seemed fine during the market, busy with his work, greeting everyone with a kind smile.

But now... now he was lying there, surrounded by the shattered remains of the things he loved most.

I took a deep breath, trying to steady the rising panic in my chest. I needed to think clearly. I needed to call for help.

My fingers fumbled for my phone. As I dialed, my mind couldn't help but race back to the strange unease I'd felt earlier—the creaking, the sense that I wasn't alone. Had someone else been awake in the lodge? Or was it just my imagination, stirred up by the obscurity of night?

"Nine-One-One." The dispatcher's voice snapped me back to the present, piercing through the silence.

I opened my mouth to speak, but the words caught in my throat. For a moment, all I could concentrate on was the faint hum of the Christmas movie still playing in the background, the sound so out of place in the midst of what I'd just found. My breath came in short, shallow bursts as I forced myself to focus. "There's... there's a man here," I finally said, my voice trembling. "I-I think he's dead. At the Christmas Lodge."

The dispatcher's voice was calm as she asked me for details, and it all felt so surreal. I stared down at Lionel's still form, the shattered ornaments around him sparkling in the firelight—the remnants of something once beautiful, now broken beyond repair.

I gave the dispatcher the information she needed, my fingers still shaking as I hung up the phone.

I took a step back, the ballroom suddenly feeling much colder than before. The warmth of the fire, the glow of the Christmas tree, it all seemed distant now, as if the magic of the night had been snuffed out by the dark reality lying at my feet.

CHAPTER FIVE

I sat at the counter, hands wrapped tightly around the mug of hot cider the lodge employee had offered me. The warmth seeped into my fingers, but it did little to chase away the cold shock that clung to me. My mind was a blur of images of Lionel's still body, the shattered ornaments, the flickering firelight casting shadows over the ballroom. I took a small sip of the cider, trying to calm the pounding in my chest.

Chief Matthew Strickland stood a few feet away, his graying brows furrowed as he spoke into his radio. His voice was calm, composed, professional.

Everything I wasn't feeling at the moment.

He glanced over at me occasionally, his stern but kind eyes softening with sympathy. The employee, a young woman whose nametag read Jessica, had been in the back room when I arrived. She sat beside me, her own mug of cider cradled in her hands.

"You did the right thing, calling it in," Jessica said softly, her voice barely above a whisper. "There is nothing else you could have done."

I nodded, but her words did little to ease the guilt that had snuck up on me as my journalistic instincts started to kick in.

Had there been something I missed? Had Lionel been suffering earlier, and I just hadn't noticed?

The questions churned in my mind, but the truth was, nothing about tonight had seemed wrong—until it suddenly was.

The sound of the lodge door swinging open cut through the quiet, and I turned just in time to see Darren and Rhett rush inside. Their boots stamped snow onto the entryway floor as they hurried toward Chief Strickland, who had just finished speaking with his team. Darren's face was a mix of concern and confusion, while Rhett skimmed his eyes nervously around the room, clearly trying to piece together what had happened.

"Dad," Darren called out as he approached, his voice tight with worry, "what's going on? What happened?"

Chief Strickland gave Darren a steady look, motioning for him to calm down before he spoke. "I was called out here after Violet found Lionel Garland in the ballroom," he said, his tone professional but with a hint of personal concern. "It appears Mr. Garland passed away. Possibly a heart attack. We'll need to wait for Curtis to confirm."

He was referring to Coroner Curtis Robinson.

Darren's face paled, and he rubbed the back of his neck, his eyes darting to me where I sat at the counter. "Violet found him?" He looked me over.

I nodded slowly, the weight of that truth sinking in all over again. "I thought he was just knocked out from what looked like a fall," I said quietly. "But when I got closer…"

Darren crossed the room in two long strides and was at my side in an instant. He rested his hand gently on my shoulder. "Are you okay?" His voice was low, full of concern.

I forced a small smile, though I knew I didn't look okay. "I'm fine. Just a little shaken up."

"Lionel? I can't believe it. He was fine earlier. I talked to him earlier tonight." Rhett moved to stand beside his uncle, his eyes wide with shock.

Chief Strickland nodded. "He seemed perfectly healthy during the event. But things like this can happen suddenly. There were no signs of trauma, no struggle. It looks like a natural death. Still, we'll have the medical examiner take a look before we come to any conclusions."

Rhett's brow furrowed. "Where's Lionel now?"

"The paramedics are with him in the ballroom," Chief Strickland replied. "They're preparing to take him to the coroner's office."

I glanced over at Darren and watched as he processed the information. The lodge was his responsibility now, and while Lionel's death wasn't connected to him in any direct way, I could see the tension in his posture. This wasn't what anyone expected on the night of the Christmas Lodge's grand reopening.

The faint sound of movement from the ballroom caught our attention. A paramedic dressed in navy-blue gear appeared at the doorway, looking solemnly at Chief Strickland. "We've got him ready for transport, Chief," the paramedic said. "Looks like a heart attack, but we'll leave that to the coroner to determine."

Chief Strickland nodded.

The paramedic turned to leave, but before he could, Darren stepped forward. "Wait," he said, his voice thick with emotion. "He…" Darren paused. "He was such an important part of this town. I just want to make sure everything's handled with respect."

The paramedic offered a sympathetic nod. "Of course, Mr. Strickland. We'll make sure he's treated with the care he deserves." He looked back toward the ballroom. "Coroner Robinson is still inside."

As the paramedic returned to the ballroom, Chief Strickland turned his attention back to us, his expression softening slightly. "I know this is hard," he said. "But for now, we need to wait for the official word from Curtis. In the meantime, it doesn't seem like the market needs to close down."

This must have been on Darren's mind, though he'd not mentioned it. Darren gave a small nod, his jaw clenched tight.

Rhett, always a bit more emotional than Darren, was clearly struggling to keep it together. He ran a hand through his dark hair, his expression revealing his worry. "I can't believe it," Rhett said, shaking his head. "I was just talking to Lionel earlier tonight."

Chief Strickland disappeared back into the ballroom, leaving me with Jessica, Darren, and Rhett.

Darren peered at me again, his hand still resting on my shoulder. "I should've been here," he murmured, more to himself than to anyone else. "I should've been here when it happened."

I shook my head. "There was nothing anyone could've done, Darren. He didn't look like he was in any distress at all during the market."

Jessica, who had been sitting quietly beside me, finally spoke up. "It's so strange," she said, her voice barely above a whisper. "Lionel was so excited earlier and was showing off the annual ornament. I can't believe he's just gone."

The room fell into somber silence, the weight of the night's events sinking in. Outside, the snow continued to fall softly, casting a sense of peace over the view through the lodge's large windows. But inside, the warmth of the evening had been replaced by the cold reality of loss.

Chief Strickland returned and cleared his throat, breaking the silence. "I'll be in touch as soon as we know more. But for now, take it easy. We'll handle things from here."

As Chief Strickland headed back into the ballroom, his heavy boots echoing on the wooden floor, I caught a glimpse of Lionel's booth in the dimly lit room beyond. My gaze drifted toward the spot where he had fallen, where the paramedics had carefully lifted his body. Everything looked mostly untouched, but... something gnawed at me.

Why are some of the ornaments so far from Lionel's body?

I replayed the possibilities in my head. If Lionel had suffered a heart attack and collapsed, maybe he'd knocked into the table on his way down. But the ornaments were scattered, some lying far from where he had been, almost behind the booth.

It didn't make sense. One glittering glass bauble was shattered near a chair that wasn't even close to the display.

How could that have happened if he had simply fallen?

A cold draft brushed against my skin, and I shivered despite the warmth of the cider in my hands. I glanced toward the large windows that lined the ballroom's far wall. Icicles hung down, sharp and glistening, catching the moonlight. But one window was slightly cracked open.

That was strange.

Who would have opened a window in this freezing weather?

I made a mental note of it but shook my head. Maybe the draft had blown some of the ornaments off the table after Lionel collapsed. Still, something didn't sit right.

"Violet?"

I turned, startled, when Jessica's soft voice broke through my thoughts. She was still sitting beside me, her hands curled around her own mug of cider. Her face was pale, her eyes wide with shock. It hit me then that she must have been almost as shaken as I was, being in the lodge when it all happened.

"Hmm?" I asked, blinking as I tried to refocus. "Sorry. What was that?"

Jessica hesitated, glancing toward the ballroom before lowering her voice. "I'm sorry."

I managed a weak smile. "Thanks. It was just so…" I paused. "Sudden. I didn't even realize something was wrong until I got close to him." I sighed, frowning.

The silence stretched between us for a moment, the loss palpable.

Curtis and the paramedics came out with the stretcher, Lionel's body inside the body bag. We all lowered our chins in respect as they passed by.

"Sorry, Darren." The chief offered his condolences. "I know you've put in a lot of time and effort the last few months for things to go smoothly. We don't know when it will be our time to die, and from the looks of everything, it was just Lionel's time."

Darren nodded his head, his lips in a fine line.

"I'm not sure who will clean up Lionel's booth, but we are all finished here." Chief Strickland put a hand on Darren's shoulder. "I'm sure word around town will spread fast when the sun pops up. Let me know if your aunt and I can do anything."

"Will do," Darren said, putting his hand on top of his dad's before the men gave each other a final, hard look.

I glanced over at Jessica, wondering what she'd been doing in the back room when everything happened. She hadn't been out here when I'd found Lionel. Had she noticed anything strange before that?

"Jessica," I said quietly, "did you hear anything before I found him? Anything unusual?"

She bit her lip, her eyes darting toward the door of the ballroom again as though she was reliving a moment in her mind. "I thought I heard something fall," she said slowly, as though unsure whether she wanted to admit it. "It was quick, just a little crash, like maybe something fell off a shelf. But I didn't think much of it at the time… I was, uh, watching a movie in the back."

My curiosity flared. "What time was that?"

"I don't know exactly," she said, frowning as she thought about it. "Maybe ten or fifteen minutes before I came out here? I didn't really notice the time until I heard you calling for help."

Jessica's words hung in the air, and I felt the knot of unease tighten in my chest. Ten or fifteen minutes before she heard me calling for help? That meant Lionel had already been lying there for at least that long, possibly longer. But why had no one noticed?

I glanced toward the ballroom again as well, my eyes narrowing at the faint reflection of the broken ornaments scattered across the floor. The eerie, cold draft from the slightly open window brushed against my skin once more, sending a shiver down my spine.

I pushed my mug of now-lukewarm cider aside and stood. "I think I'm going to take a look at the ballroom again," I said, more to myself than to Jessica. I made my way toward the room without waiting for her response.

The flickering light from the Christmas tree in the lobby reached into the ballroom, casting long dancing shadows across the floor. The festive decorations seemed in stark contrast to the heaviness in my chest as I stepped inside. The room was quiet save for the faint ticking of the old grandfather clock in the corner and the muffled voices of the paramedics preparing Lionel's body for transport.

I moved closer to the booth where I had found Lionel, careful to avoid stepping on any broken glass. From this angle, it all looked so surreal. His booth had been pristine earlier that evening, every ornament precisely placed, every decoration in order. But now, the scene was in chaos, shattered ornaments and broken toys scattered far beyond where his body had lain.

I crouched down, studying the floor. The glass from one of the shattered ornaments was lying near a display two booths over, way too far from Lionel's booth to have been knocked over if he'd fallen. My pulse quickened.

Had someone thrown it? Or had something or someone knocked it over in the minutes before Lionel collapsed?

I examined the possibilities over and over in my mind. How could the ornaments have ended up so far away from where his body had been? Something didn't add up.

The ballroom was quiet now, the festive decorations and twinkling lights at odds with the unsettling scene before me. Everything looked out of place.

Everything had been perfectly arranged earlier, but now the booth was in disarray. They had taken away Lionel's body, but the mess remained, with broken glass and toppled decorations creating chaos.

I moved closer to one of the fallen ornaments, kneeling down to study the way it had shattered. The glass glittered in the soft light, and my mind raced with questions.

If Lionel had collapsed, his fall might have knocked a few things over, but this? No. The damage covered too much area, and the ornaments were scattered too far from where I'd discovered his body.

I glanced around the room, my eyes narrowing as I tried to make sense of the scene. The ornaments had somehow ended up on the floor, but there was no obvious reason for it. They were shattered, some even several feet away from the booth.

It made little sense.

The thunk-tap of my boots echoed in the vast ballroom, but then the sound was swallowed by a thick rug beneath my feet. As I reached the spot where his head had been, I froze.

A rug.

"A rug!" I yelled, causing everyone to turn and look at me as though I was crazy. "Darren, go get your dad. Hurry."

Darren knew I was on to something, and I was, but I didn't know what.

Yet.

I stood still, not saying a word, but it wasn't long until Chief Strickland and Darren were back in the ballroom.

"Hear me out," I said, lifting my hands before they could interrupt. "Look where I found Lionel's body. His head was right here." I pointed to the spot on the floor.

Chief Strickland nodded, his eyes following my finger.

"Now, look at where the ornaments are. They're scattered too far away," I continued, stepping toward the shards. "If Lionel collapsed, sure, he might have knocked a few things over, but he wouldn't have sent ornaments flying several feet across the room... And he was on a rug," I added, my voice sharp.

I picked up one of the less expensive ornaments from Lionel's display and threw it on the floor with force. It landed on the thick rug with a dull thud but didn't break.

"I threw that hard, and it still didn't shatter," I pointed out. "Yet these"—I gestured to the broken glass scattered across the floor—"have been shattered."

I walked over to where the ornament had rolled and noted it was near the spot where Lionel's head had rested on the floor. "Even if they had rolled, they wouldn't have shattered." I stopped talking when the toe of my boot made a squishy sound.

"What?" the chief asked.

I rocked back and forth, feeling the rug clearly saturated with something beneath my feet.

I looked around at my surroundings, considering what I wanted to say. "Wasn't his head here?" I asked for clarification.

"Yes," Chief Strickland confirmed. He then pulled his notebook from his pocket to double check. "Yes."

"Did Lionel have any wounds or foaming at the mouth?" I knew both were possible after death or a hard hit to the head. "Because there is a wet spot of something here. Where his head was." I clarified because I didn't want them to assume it was urine or another such bodily fluid that is often released during a person's final moments.

The chief hurried over and tugged his flashlight out of his utility belt to confirm the rug was indeed wet.

He put up his hand for me to step back then took his phone out of his pocket and put in a call to Curtis Robinson, asking him to turn around and come back.

"And I noticed the window is cracked open." I pointed.

"Cracked?" Darren's eyes lifted. "Those should be locked tight. I checked them myself."

"That one's not." I shrugged.

Both men walked over. Darren was about to shut the window, but I saw Chief Strickland gesture for him to leave it alone, a move I took as confirmation something strange must have taken place.

"Good catch," Darren said to me after Chief Strickland moved us out of the ballroom and told us to stay put.

"Darren, I think someone killed him." My words made Darren's face turn as white as the snow that was outside.

"No." He shook his head, refusing to believe my statement. "That can't be. That did not happen. I do not care how many bodies of murder victims you have found. This is not one of them."

"It's totally one of them, so you better get an idea of what you're going to do in the morning when folks start turning up here to shop at the indoor Christmas market," I said.

The air was tense, and neither of us uttered another word.

That was, until Curtis Robinson returned for a few minutes with his little black bag to collect some samples from the carpet where Lionel had lain.

"I've never seen this done before," I said, referring to the investigational process, "which only proves to me that I'm right. Lionel Garland was murdered."

CHAPTER SIX

Lucky for me, the village was good about salting and clearing the roads. Otherwise, I'd have slipped and slid all the way down the mountain this morning, nearly breaking my neck just to get to work.

I rushed out the door of my apartment, bundled against the freezing air, just in time to see the trolley coming up the hill. It squeaked to a stop in front of me, and before I could take a step, the door whipped open.

"Well, look what the cat dragged in." Goldie Bennett's voice rang out like a bell, her bejeweled visor flashing brightly as the tiny Christmas lights embedded in it blinked out a rhythm. Her round face was framed by a mass of perfectly styled hair—blond with a bit of sparkle, just like the rest of her. "You gonna stand there, freezing, or are you getting on? I ain't got all day, Missy."

I grinned despite the cold biting at my face. Goldie was a whirlwind of energy and gossip, and there wasn't a soul in Holiday Junction who could get through a conversation with her without hearing about her grandchildren, the latest town drama, or what some random tourist said about the hot cocoa at Brewing Beans.

"I'm coming. I'm coming." I laughed, stepping onto the trolley just before she yanked the door shut behind me with her usual enthusiasm. She barely waited for me to sit down before jerking the trolley back into motion, sending me sliding down the bench a couple of inches.

"You look like you've seen a ghost, girl. What's the matter with you?" Goldie shot a glance over her shoulder, expertly steering the trolley with one hand and adjusting her sparkling visor with the other. "Or did that Darren Strickland finally put a ring on it?"

I nearly choked on the hot air I was blowing into my hands to warm them. "No, nothing like that," I said, sitting up straighter and giving her a half-smile. "Just... a lot happened last night. Found Lionel Garland—"

"Dead?" Goldie interrupted, whipping the trolley around a corner so fast I had to grab the rail to keep from sliding again. "I heard some rumblin's this morning but didn't catch all the details. Spill it, honey! You know I've got my ear to the ground. Didn't think I'd be hearing about *that* on my route today though."

I shook my head, recognizing the familiar buzz of small-town gossip rising. Goldie loved to keep up with all the goings-on in Holiday Junction, and if there was anything to be known, Goldie knew it—thanks to her trolley passengers, of course.

"I'm not sure what happened yet," I said cautiously. "Chief Strickland thinks it might've been a heart attack. But..." I hesitated, glancing at her out of the corner of my eye.

Goldie wasn't fooled for a second. "But you're not so sure, are ya?" She grinned, showing a flash of white teeth. "A gal like you's always pokin' her nose where it don't belong—and I mean that in the nicest way, of course. Got that keen reporter sense, don'tcha?"

"I don't know, Goldie," I admitted, leaning back as the trolley rattled along the snow-covered streets. "Something about it feels... off. There were some things that didn't make sense. I'm heading to the *Junction Journal* now to go over what I've got and maybe put together a piece, but... I don't know. Something's just not sitting right with me."

"Well, sugar, you can count on me to keep my ear to the ground," Goldie assured me with a wink, her visor lights blinking in sync with her words. "Ain't nothing slips past the trolley route, I tell ya. I'll hear all about it soon enough, and you'll be the first to know if anything juicy comes up."

I smiled, feeling a little lighter. Goldie had a way of turning any conversation into a lively one, and even though the weight of Lionel's death was still pressing on me, it was nice to have someone on my side—even if her approach was a little more... colorful.

As we rumbled down the seaside road, I caught sight of my office—a cozy clapboard house nestled beyond the dunes, its roof dusted with snow. The *Junction Journal* had been my refuge ever since I arrived in Holiday Junction, and despite its creaky floorboards and drafty windows, it was home. And it was the perfect place to unravel whatever mystery lay ahead.

Goldie pulled the trolley to a stop in front of the office, jerking the door open with her usual flair. "Alright, sweetheart, here's your stop," she said, flashing me a knowing look. "You go solve whatever mystery's gnawing at ya. And don't be surprised if you hear some rumors by lunchtime—I'll be keeping folks talkin'."

I stepped off the trolley, my boots crunching in the snow, and turned to give Goldie one last wave before she rolled down the street, visor blinking away like a beacon of holiday cheer.

As the trolley rolled away, I turned toward the *Junction Journal* office, which was nestled just behind the dunes. The seaside winds whipped through my hair, carrying the salty, crisp air of the ocean. Even though winter had settled over Holiday Junction, the beach remained stunning in its cold, windswept beauty. The sky above the sea was a soft gray-blue, and the waves crashed against the shore, their foamy white tips glistening under the overcast sky. I pulled my coat tighter around me as the chilly sea breeze tugged at the edges of my scarf.

The light on Darren's lighthouse rotated all along the seaside, and I smiled, trying to only think of the romantic night last night, before things had turned.

The small clapboard cottage that housed the *Junction Journal* was decorated in full Christmas cheer. A festive wreath made of seashells, starfish, and sprigs of evergreen hung on the windows, while garlands of holly wrapped around the porch rails.

On the front porch stood a charming little Christmas tree, dressed up in a seaside theme, tiny ornaments shaped like lighthouses, seashells, and shimmering blue bulbs. The whole scene looked like something out of a coastal Christmas postcard.

I smiled as I caught sight of Mama's signature golf cart parked haphazardly in the small driveway in front of the office, a few red ribbons tied around the roof rails for holiday flair. The cart was barely visible from within the enclosure she'd added to keep her warm and toasty.

But what really caught my attention was the large white van parked next to it. The vehicle looked suspiciously like a news van, complete with a satellite dish mounted on top. The glossy exterior had a sleek appearance.

"What in the world…" I murmured to myself, squinting at the van as I crossed the snowy path leading to the front porch. The van's logo was tastefully subtle but still screamed high-end media.

I paused on the porch, glancing over my shoulder toward the outline of the mountain where the Christmas Lodge and the art district sat nestled. Even in the dim light of a winter morning, I could make out the shape of the mountain looming in the distance. From down here, I couldn't see the lodge itself or the market, but the faint outline of the snow-covered trees and rooftops was unmistakable against the gray sky.

With a deep breath, I turned back to the cottage, the scent of saltwater mingling with the faint hint of pine from the garland. As soon as I pushed open the front door, a rush of warmth hit me, and with it, the soft strains of Christmas music playing in the background. "It's Beginning to Look a Lot Like Christmas" floated through the air, accompanied by the sound of soft laughter from the back of the office, where the kitchen was located.

The rich, inviting smells of fresh coffee and something sweet like cinnamon and sugar drifted toward me, making my mouth water.

I walked down the hall, unsure of what to expect.

I hadn't been prepared for company this morning, and the presence of the van outside had thrown me off.

I rounded the corner into the kitchen area and came face-to-face with a surprising scene: my mama was sitting at the employee kitchen table, beaming from ear to ear, holding what appeared to be a festive Christmas donut for breakfast.

The table was scattered with more of the same—brightly colored donuts decorated with red and green icing, some shaped like Christmas trees and some like snowflakes. I knew those donuts came from Sugarbrush Bakery.

But it wasn't just Mama at the table. Two strangers, a man and a woman, both dressed stylishly for the season, were sitting beside her, sipping coffee from the *Journal*'s mismatched mugs and looking every bit at ease in the cozy kitchen.

The man wore a crisp navy jacket with a scarf draped casually around his neck, while the woman sported a chic winter coat and matching leather gloves.

"Violet, sweetheart!" Mama's voice rang out, full of excitement as she jumped up from her chair and waved me over. "I want you to meet these fine folks."

I blinked in surprise, taking a moment to process the scene before I walked over. The smell of those Christmas donuts was intoxicating, and the kitchen was filled with the cheerful glow of twinkling lights strung along the cabinets. A small tabletop tree sat in the corner, its tiny ornaments sparkling.

"These lovely people are from *Southern Charm* magazine," Mama declared proudly, her Southern drawl even thicker because of her excitement. She gestured to the couple seated at the table. "This here is Jeffrey, and this is Annalise. They're the ones doing the feature on the lodge reopening. Isn't it just the most wonderful thing?"

I felt my eyebrows shoot up in surprise. *Southern Charm* magazine? The same magazine that had been covering the grand opening last night? I offered the couple a polite smile, feeling the weight of their unexpected visit. "It's a pleasure to meet you," I said, my voice polite but tinged with curiosity. "I didn't realize we had such special guests today."

"Oh, darling, we've been having the best time. I'm just thrilled they brought us these amazing donuts," Mama said with a wave of her hand, as though she hadn't just dropped a bombshell. "We're just going over all the details for the spread. They wanted to get a real feel for the town, you know? And what better place to start than right here at the *Junction Journal*?"

Jeffrey, the man in the navy jacket, smiled warmly at me, his eyes twinkling with the same holiday cheer that seemed to radiate from every corner of the office. "Your mother has been an absolute delight," he said in a smooth, easy tone. "We're thrilled to be covering such a charming town. And the Christmas Lodge, well, that's the crown jewel, isn't it?"

Annalise, the woman seated next to him, nodded in agreement, her elegant features lighting up. "We couldn't resist coming down to see everything for ourselves after we got the email about how festive the village is. Holiday Junction is... magical, really. We're hoping to capture that magic in our feature."

"Well, you certainly picked the right time to visit," I said, glancing around at the decorations that filled every nook and cranny of the cottage. My mama had really gone all out this year. "It's always something special around here during the holidays."

Mama practically glowed with pride, clearly thrilled to have such prestigious guests in our midst. "I told them, Violet, I told them that you would be the perfect person to talk to about the village and all its wonderful traditions. You've been covering Holiday Junction as the head of the paper now for a few years. No one is more perfect. And before I forget, each one of the Blackwell sisters called and left a message about you featuring them in the Christmas Market."

I couldn't help but smile. Betty, Beatrice, and Belle Blackwell had taken out a big ad in the *Junction Journal* to be featured over the weekend for their Jingle and Mingle booth at the Christmas Market.

"I'll go see them today," I said and then turned my attention to the guests. "I'd be happy to help you however I can." My mind was already racing with thoughts of what this feature could mean for the town and for me.

"Mama"—I looked over at her—"do you have the morning stats?" This was her cue to mosey on out of there and start her job as the office assistant. That was what she did when she wasn't working at her Leisure Center or volunteering with the Leading Ladies.

"A paper never sleeps," she said and got up. "It was so nice to meet you two. I'm sure I'll see you at all the festivities this week."

Mama gave a wink and wiggled her fingers in a goodbye before disappearing down the hall toward the office she shared with Radley. I watched her go, still trying to wrap my head around the scene I'd walked into. *Southern Charm* magazine doing a spread on the Christmas Lodge was big enough news, but it was hard to stay focused with Lionel Garland's death weighing heavily on my mind.

Speaking of Radley—I glanced up at the clock, mentally checking the time. He wasn't scheduled to come in until later this morning, right around the time I'd be leaving the office to report on some of the festival activities. I'd almost forgotten that I was supposed to cover more events today, what with everything that had happened last night. My thoughts were a swirling mix of why Jeffrey and Annalise were really here and, of course, Lionel's sudden death.

"Your mother is sweet." Annalise's voice broke into my thoughts, drawing my attention back to her. There was something about the way she said it—polite but direct—that made it clear she wasn't Southern. Her next words only confirmed it. "But let's cut to the chase. We know there was a murder last night. And that you found the body."

I blinked, the words hitting me like one of those icy kinda snowballs. Hard, stingy, and cold.

"Whoa," I blurted, putting my hands up defensively, the words coming out before I could stop them. "Who on earth would say such a thing?"

Jeffrey leaned back in his chair, crossing his arms over his chest in a way that said he wasn't buying my innocent act. "We're staying at the lodge, Violet. We heard the rumblings first thing this morning—people talking in hushed tones, whispers about a body being found. Naturally, we started asking around."

"And we heard you were the one who found him," Annalise added, her gaze sharp and unyielding. "We came here to do a spread on the lodge's reopening, but this? A murder in the middle of a Christmas festival? This is much bigger than a feature about a holiday event. We're talking international coverage."

My heart raced, and I could feel my pulse thumping in my throat. A murder? International coverage? I wasn't sure whether to laugh or scream. The truth was, they weren't completely wrong. Lionel's death was suspicious, and the more I thought about it, the less it felt like a simple heart attack. But I wasn't about to let *Southern Charm* swoop in and steal the story—especially not a couple of out-of-towners who didn't know Holiday Junction the way I did.

I forced a polite smile, though my insides were churning. "Look, I don't know where you're getting your information, but I wouldn't jump to conclusions. There's been no official word about a murder."

"Oh, come on," Annalise pressed, leaning forward slightly. "You know better than that. Where there's smoke, there's fire. We've been in this business long enough to recognize a story when we see one. And this?" She gestured vaguely, her eyes gleaming with the thrill of the chase. "This is going to blow up. A charming Christmas village, an iconic lodge reopening, and a murder at the center of it all? People will eat this up."

As I listened to her, the pit in my stomach grew deeper. It wasn't just what she was saying, but how she was saying it. There was a hunger in her voice, a raw ambition that I recognized all too well—because I used to have it. Before Holiday Junction, back when I'd been chasing the next big story, I would have done anything to get a scoop like this. I would have fought tooth and nail to be the one to break it, to see my name splashed across the front page of every major outlet.

But that was before. Before I'd come to this little town and discovered something far more important than the chase for fame. This place had changed me, and I'd thought I'd left that cutthroat side of myself behind. But hearing Annalise talk like this, watching her and Jeffrey strategize their way into making this murder the biggest story of the year, stirred something deep and unsettling inside me.

If they think they're going to come in here and steal that scoop right out from under me... I clenched my fists under the table, my nails digging into my palms. The thought scared me because it wasn't who I was anymore. But the temptation was there, like an old ghost haunting me, whispering that I could outmaneuver them, get ahead, and take back what I'd always wanted.

But no. I wasn't that person anymore. I couldn't be. I'd worked too hard to build something different here in Holiday Junction, to leave that version of me behind. Still, the idea of losing this story to two opportunistic reporters made my stomach twist in ways I didn't want to acknowledge.

I glanced at the clock again, feeling the weight of their gazes on me. I had to tread carefully. One wrong move, and they'd sniff out the fact that something bigger was at play—and if I wasn't careful, they'd get the story of a lifetime.

My story.

With a deep breath, I forced another tight smile. "Like I said, there's no official word on anything yet. I think you might be jumping the gun here. But you're welcome to stick around Holiday Junction and enjoy the festival—there's plenty of other stories here that don't involve wild rumors."

Jeffrey and Annalise exchanged a look, clearly unconvinced, but neither of them pushed further. For now.

"Of course," Jeffrey said smoothly, his smile tight. "We wouldn't want to spread rumors, not having all the facts."

But I could see it in his eyes. They weren't leaving this alone. And the truth was, neither was I.

Heavy footsteps came down the hall, shaking me from my swirling thoughts. The sound of the office doorbell ringing must have been drowned out by the ringing in my ears from the frustration building inside me. When Radley strolled into the kitchen, I almost felt a surge of relief. Maybe I could pawn these two off on him and buy myself some time to think.

"Hey," he greeted with a grin, tugging off his stocking cap and shaking the snow from his shoulders. "I see you've met Annalise." He waved his hand as if he, Jeffrey, and Annalise were old friends catching up after years apart. "Isn't she great? And what about Violet, huh?" Radley nodded in my direction, clearly in good spirits. "I told you that you would love this place."

"Wait," I said, trying to process this. "You know them? You're the one who got *Southern Charm* to come here?"

Radley shook his head, a bit too casual for my liking. "Nope, not me," he said.

"It was Evelyn Frost," Annalise chimed in, flipping through her notes like it was all old news. "Now *there* is a character," she added, glancing at Jeffrey for confirmation.

"Evelyn Frost?" The name immediately sparked something in me. Evelyn ran a quaint little shop in town, full of her hand-painted ornaments and artisan crafts. She was a staple in the art community but eccentric, to say the least.

"Yep." Annalise nodded, continuing, "When we

emailed to tell her we were coming to do the piece on the lodge and her design winning the annual ornament competition, she emailed back and pleaded with us not to come." She paused, raising an eyebrow. "Of course, that only made us more curious."

Jeffrey nodded, jumping in. "Yeah, we showed up anyway. When we went to her shop, she wasn't exactly rolling out the welcome mat. Turns out she didn't win the annual ornament competition this year. Mr. Garland did. And, let's just say, she was shocked we were still planning to do the feature after that."

"She didn't even wait to chat," Annalise added with a chuckle. "Practically ran out of her own studio. Left us standing there."

That little nugget of information lodged itself firmly in my mind, and I tucked it away to explore later. Evelyn losing the competition was interesting, but her dramatic reaction to them being here was even more intriguing.

Jeffrey stood up and walked over to Radley before draping an arm around him with the easy camaraderie of someone who knew him well. "And we go way back, of course. Worked with Radley here for years before he got cozy in this charming little town." He smirked, glancing back at me. "And that cute redhead up there at the bakery."

"He was always attracted to the redheads," Annalise joked.

"When we started poking around about the murder," Jeffrey continued, "we saw Radley's name on the *Junction Journal* website and called him up."

Radley chuckled, shaking his head. "Listen, I'm not that old." He shot Jeffrey a playful glare before turning to me with a grin. "But I did tell them one thing for sure and that was how you, Violet Rhinehammer, have an uncanny knack for sniffing out crimes and killers."

The compliment from Radley caught me off guard. I couldn't help but feel a mix of pride and unease at the praise. I had tried to leave that life behind, the one where chasing down criminals and headlines consumed me. And yet, here I was, not only getting tangled up in another mystery but, apparently, with a reputation for it.

"Between the three of you"—Radley's finger swept over me, Jeffrey, and Annalise—"you'll have this murder wrapped up before Chief Strickland can get the autopsy report back."

"And your charming little village will have the best spread you've ever seen from any magazine," Annalise added, her gaze sharp, "and possibly"—she paused, locking eyes with Jeffrey—"a feature story on national news."

"Whooooweee!" Mama's voice rang out from

somewhere nearby. I was sure she'd had her ears pinned to our conversation the whole time. She appeared in the kitchen doorway, hands clapping together, her eyes gleaming with excitement. "We could use some big national news to get even more tourists here. Just think," she gushed, "Darren's Christmas Lodge will be booked solid all year long!"

Dang it.

Of course Mama had to bring up Darren. Not only throw him into the conversation but also talk about how this whole situation could give his lodge a boost. Her voice was filled with pride and excitement, the wheels in her head already spinning with visions of bustling tourists, busy shops, and Holiday Junction becoming the next big holiday destination. She was all but handing the story over on a silver platter.

I bit my lip, frustration building as I tried to keep my face neutral. Now I had no other choice.

I had been so careful. Ever since I'd moved to Holiday Junction, I'd kept my old cutthroat instincts in check. This town wasn't the cutthroat world of big-city journalism—it was my fresh start. A place where I could breathe, slow down, and let go of the relentless hunger for a scoop. But now, with Radley's compliment, Jeffrey and Annalise circling the story like vultures, and Mama unknowingly stoking the fire by dangling Darren's lodge in front of them… I felt the old drive creeping back in, whispering in my ear. *If you don't act fast, they're going to take this right out from under you.*

I didn't like that old drive because I didn't want to be that person anymore. But there it was, gnawing at the back of my mind. If I didn't stay ahead of them, this story—my story—would be theirs. And they were already getting too close to the truth.

I forced a smile, feeling tension pulling at the edges of it. "National news?" I repeated, playing along. "That's... a big deal."

"Exactly," Jeffrey said, leaning in as if he were about to uncover a big secret. "This is more than just a charming little lodge story now. This is murder in a place where people come for holiday cheer. It'll go viral in no time. People will be talking about this for weeks."

Mama looked like she was about to burst with joy at the idea, already picturing the attention the town would get. But I couldn't let that happen. Not this way.

"Right," I said, choosing my words carefully. "But I think we need to be mindful here. We don't have all the facts yet, and we don't want to jump to conclusions before Chief Strickland's had a chance to investigate properly."

Jeffrey and Annalise exchanged a look, their faces still brimming with excitement. They weren't backing down. I could see the fire in their eyes—they were already smelling the ink of the headline.

"And until then," I added, straightening up and looking at Radley, "we'll just have to wait and see what the investigation turns up. No rushing in with half the story."

Radley raised an eyebrow at me, as if sensing the tension bubbling under my calm exterior. But he didn't say anything, just gave me a slow nod as if to say, *I get it, but this is your mess to handle.*

"Of course," Annalise said, the smile never leaving her face. "We wouldn't dream of writing anything until the facts are clear."

I didn't believe that for a second.

"My understanding is that you're here to do an article on the ornament and the festival, not a death," I said.

"We can do both," Jeffrey responded. "In fact, we are contractors for the magazine and we can submit any reports to the wire."

"We are always looking for the next big scoop, but you're right," Annalise said, appearing as if she were about to cover their tracks. "We are definitely here to shine a spotlight on Holiday Junction, not just the ornament."

"I just know this is going to be huge. Holiday Junction is going to be *the* place to be!" Mama clapped her hands again, practically vibrating with enthusiasm.

I swallowed the rising frustration, forcing myself to keep the smile on my face. This story, whatever it was turning into, was about to become much bigger than I wanted it to be. And now, thanks to Mama and Darren's lodge, I had no other choice but to make sure I stayed ahead of it.

Because the last thing I wanted was for journalists from *Southern Charm* to get the scoop of a lifetime—especially if it involved more than just a lodge feature.

CHAPTER SEVEN

Everyone was quiet, silently calculating their next move. I felt trapped, standing at a crossroads between my journalistic instincts and the life I'd built here in Holiday Junction. Annalise and Jeffrey's eyes flickered with ambition, but I had no intention of letting them turn my town into a media circus.

The kettle in the kitchen whistled suddenly, breaking the tension and startling me. I seized the opportunity, walking over to pour myself a cup of tea, trying to keep my hands steady. I needed a moment to gather my thoughts.

Radley, sensing my need for a distraction, cleared his throat. "Well, we should probably head out," he said, nudging Jeffrey lightly with his elbow. "I've got a meeting later today, and you guys are probably itching to check out the Christmas Market, right?"

Annalise gave a wry smile, her sharp eyes never leaving mine. "Of course. We wouldn't want to miss it." Her tone was casual, but I could sense the undercurrent in her words. She was onto something, and it was only a matter of time before she pieced together the rest.

Mama beamed, clearly oblivious to the tension in the room. "Oh, you'll love it. The market is one of the best parts of the festival," she said, bouncing on her toes. "You'll find all sorts of beautiful crafts, handmade ornaments, and of course, the best hot chocolate this side of the Mississippi."

"I'm sure we will," Annalise replied smoothly, standing up from her seat and pulling her leather gloves back on. She turned to me, her eyes narrowing just slightly. "Violet, we'll be in touch. I'm sure we'll see each other again before too long."

"Yeah." I nodded, managing a tight smile. "I'm sure we will."

Annalise and Jeffrey bid their goodbyes and made their way out the door, leaving Radley and me in an awkward silence. The tension that had been building all morning seemed to dissipate as soon as they left, but it was replaced by a gnawing unease.

Radley stuffed his hands into his pockets, rocking back on his heels. "Well, that was… something."

I snorted, leaning against the counter. "Something? I'm not sure why you would volunteer me."

"Yeah, sorry about that. I didn't even think." He shook his head and walked over to push in the chair where Jeffrey had been sitting. "He left his bag." He grabbed the black leather satchel and ran out of the kitchen in the hopes of catching them.

"Are you okay?" Mama asked and brought a napkin from the kitchen counter to place in front of me.

"I've got to deal with them sniffing around, and Lionel's death..." I trailed off, shaking my head.

"This will make you feel better," Mama said confidently, picking out one of the donuts shaped like a Christmas tree and decorated with icing string lights, round balls of candy as ornaments, and a big gold icing star. "You really think there's more to it than just a heart attack, don't you?" Mama asked.

I nodded, my thoughts returning to the strange scene in the ballroom. "I do. Something doesn't feel right. The broken ornaments, the wet spot near Lionel's body. It doesn't add up. And now, with Annalise and Jeffrey poking around, I feel like we're running out of time to figure it out before this blows up."

"Well, you've got my help if you need it. I'm pretty good at figuring stuff out," Mama said. "Just like when you was a wily teenager and thought I didn't know you were sneaking out of your room."

"I never did ask you how you figured that out." I eyeballed her.

"I was watering my lilies I'd planted around that awful air conditioning unit outside of your bedroom window. And when I noticed the outdoor outlet next to it was starting to come away from the wall, it didn't take much smarts to see it was probably a good placement for a foot to hoist you in and out that window of yours." Mama laughed.

I did too.

"I still remember your face when you were crawling back in and looked up to see me sittin' on your bed." Mama sighed, a satisfied look on her face. "And there's got to be something with that wet spot you found next to Lionel's head. I don't know what, but I bet I can figure it out."

"You just might be right." I sucked in a deep breath and only relaxed when my teeth sank into that delicious Sugarbrush Bakery donut.

"Dang it. I missed them." Radley came back into the kitchen, snowflakes resting on his shoulders and flecks in his hair. "I called them but didn't get an answer, so I left a message on his phone to tell him it's here."

"Thanks, Radley," I said.

"Well, Radley, we are gonna investigate the suspicion around Lionel's death before them folks." Mama practically danced around the kitchen, oblivious to the worry etched across my face.

Radley even offered a hand, and Mama took it, leading them both into a little twirl.

"Mama," I said gently, trying to rein her in. "We need to be careful. There's a lot more going on than you realize."

"What do you mean?" Radley stopped mid-twirl, his eyes narrowing with concern.

I took a deep breath, deciding to fill him in on the details of Lionel's death.

"There are some things that don't make sense about Lionel's passing. It may not have been just a heart attack. There's a chance"—I paused and took a deep breath—"there's a chance it could have been foul play."

"That's what we need to figure out," Radley said. "If there's a big scoop to be had, let's just say Jeffrey and Annalisa will not let it go. And that's why I'm in Holiday Junction."

"Then let's get going." Mama wasted no time. She grabbed the box of donuts. "Radley, get the coffee."

She gestured with a tilt of her head for me to follow her into my office.

As we entered my office, I couldn't help but glance out the large window that overlooked the dunes, stretching out toward the seaside. The usual serenity of the beach was now accented with the energy of holiday festivities. Despite the cold, I could see children bundled up in coats and scarves, building sandmen—snowmen made of sand, a local holiday tradition—and people milling about in the distance, preparing for the day's Christmas Market.

A list of Christmas Market events was scrawled across the whiteboard in the corner, but what immediately caught my attention was a new list on the adjacent whiteboard labeled "Christmas Lodge Festivities."

My brows furrowed in surprise as I looked at the neatly written schedule. "Mama," I asked, turning to her, "did you put this up?"

"Oh, honey, of course I did," Mama said with a proud smile, setting a box of donuts down on my desk. "I came in early this morning and thought we should keep track of all the big goings-on at the lodge, especially since you had no idea what Darren was up to up there. We've got to stay ahead of it all for the Junction Journal, don't we?"

I took another look at the whiteboards she'd set up around my desk, covered with neatly penned events and descriptions, all scheduled over the next few weeks. It hit me that my sleuthing would have to be squeezed between these festivities if I hoped to keep the Journal's readers up-to-date. I skimmed down the list of holiday events in awe of just how much Holiday Junction had planned.

At the heart of town, the Holiday Junction Snowflake Parade would kick things off, with floats, performers, and even Santa himself parading down Peppermint Court. I could already imagine the glittering lights, the children's excited faces, and Santa's booming "ho-ho-ho" echoing through the streets.

Next up, Sugarbrush Bakery would be hosting its Gingerbread House Competition. That was always a highlight—the villagers and tourists would be elbow-deep in frosting and gumdrops, creating miniature masterpieces to be judged by none other than our own Mayor Paisley. Then, over at Brewing Beans, the town's best cocoa recipes would face off in the Hot Cocoa Contest. The coveted Mug of the Year was on the line, and I'd be lying if I said I wasn't excited to sample the contenders.

For those with a creative flair, there was an Ornament Crafting Booth down by the beach where local artisans would be teaching children—and a few eager adults, I'm sure—how to make their own ornaments out of seashells, pinecones, and a touch of Christmas magic. And not far from there, the Snowman Sand Sculpting Contest would take place. Only in Holiday Junction would you find snowmen made out of sand, complete with scarves and hats.

Families would have their hands full with the

Holiday Scavenger Hunt. The town was hiding clues everywhere, and treasures were tucked into every nook and cranny. It would all end with a grand prize reveal at the lodge itself, making it a true adventure. And as the sun set, the Seaside Christmas Carol Sing-Along would gather people by the dunes, their voices rising with the crash of the waves and ending in a candlelight procession to Celebration Park.

Of course, the jolly old man himself would be visiting, too. Santa would make his way to Celebration Park for photos and story time, and a little holiday fair would pop up right after. Children's laughter would fill the air, mixing with the aroma of roasted chestnuts and caramel corn.

And that was only in town. The Christmas Lodge was pulling out all the stops too. The grand Tree Lighting Ceremony was scheduled, with fireworks, caroling, and a performance by the ever-spirited Mad Fiddlers. Inside the lodge, the Annual Christmas Ornament Auction would showcase Lionel Garland's rare vintage pieces, all going toward the town's holiday fund.

I couldn't help but smile at the thought of the Cookie Decorating Workshop in the lodge's ballroom. The smell of fresh-baked sugar cookies would drift through the air, and holiday music would play softly as people decorated with sprinkles and icing. And as if that weren't cozy enough, there was an Ice

Skating and Cocoa Night planned at the lodge's pond. Skaters would glide under the stars, warming up with hot cocoa by the bonfire afterward.

Not to be outdone, the lodge would also host a Holiday Wreath-Making Class, inviting people to craft beautiful wreaths from local greenery, ribbons, and ornaments. And for those with a little more energy, the annual Snowball Tournament would take place on the front lawn. Teams would battle for the title of "Snowball Champions," and I could already imagine the laughter and the rosy cheeks.

The sheer number of events made me feel like Christmas was bubbling over in every corner of Holiday Junction. I'd have to work fast to keep up with it all for the Journal—and maybe, just maybe, Darren and I could sneak in a few quiet holiday moments of our own.

"It looks like number two at the lodge has a much different meaning now," I said.

My mind raced with thoughts of the unexpected developments surrounding Lionel Garland's death. It was hard to concentrate on the festive cheer when something so serious was simmering beneath the surface.

"Mama, this is a lot. How am I supposed to juggle all of this and the other things going on?" I asked, feeling the weight of the responsibility pressing down on me.

"Don't you worry about a thing, sweetheart," Mama said, reaching over and giving my shoulder a reassuring squeeze. "You focus on what you need to. Radley and I will handle the rest of the festival coverage for the paper."

Radley caught my eye as he poured coffee into one of the mugs. "Violet," he said quietly, "we've got your back. But we can't ignore the fact that Lionel's death is starting to look more complicated than just a heart attack. If there's something there, we'll find it."

I gave him a grateful nod, the warm scents of cinnamon donuts and freshly brewed coffee momentarily easing the knot in my chest. But I knew that the clock was ticking. The lodge was set to host some of the biggest events of the season, and with *Southern Charm*'s reporters sniffing around, I had to stay on top of everything—both for the sake of the *Junction Journal* and to uncover the truth of what really happened to Lionel Garland.

"Then it's settled," I said, straightening up, determination settling in. "We'll stay on top of the festival and the investigation. But let's do it quietly... I don't want anyone jumping to conclusions before we have any solid proof."

Radley gave a firm nod, and Mama offered one last encouraging smile before handing me a steaming mug of coffee. I could see the wheels turning in her head, already strategizing her next move.

"First things first," Mama said, pulling her phone out with a quick flourish. She snapped a couple of photos of the whiteboard—capturing the list of Christmas Market events and the recently added Christmas Lodge board. Then, with a swift, no-nonsense exchange, she traded her phone for the dry erase marker.

"We need a murder board," she declared, a twinkle of excitement in her eyes.

I nearly choked on my coffee, sputtering as I set it down on the edge of my desk. "A what?" I coughed, looking at her in disbelief.

"A murder board, honey," Mama said, as if it were the most obvious thing in the world. "You know, like they do in all those detective shows. We need a visual aid to keep track of everything. This way, we can start piecing it all together—like Lionel's timeline, people's whereabouts, clues." She motioned to the blank section of the board with a wave of her hand. "It'll help us keep our heads straight."

Radley chuckled as Mama expertly wiped a clean space on the whiteboard next to the festival schedule and Christmas Lodge events. "She's got a point, Violet. Might help organize everything while keeping things... discreet."

"I'm not sure 'discreet' is in Mama's vocabulary," I muttered, but deep down, I had to admit the idea had merit. If we were going to get to the bottom of what really happened to Lionel, we'd need to keep things organized, especially with all the holiday events going on. And with Jeffrey and Annalise sniffing around, any leg up we had could help keep the story in our hands.

Mama uncapped the dry erase marker, her face lit up with excitement. "Okay," she said, her voice brimming with authority. "Let's start with the basics."

She began to write "Victim: Lionel Garland" in bold letters at the top of the board, followed by "Cause of Death: TBD" beneath it.

"We know Lionel was found at the Christmas Lodge," I said, my mind spinning as I recounted the events of last night. "We don't yet know for sure what caused his death, but the circumstances were... strange."

"Suspicious," Mama corrected, writing the word in a big circle beside Lionel's name.

"Right. Suspicious," I agreed, glancing over at Radley. "The broken ornaments scattered around his booth. The open window. And that wet spot near his head."

Radley nodded, crossing his arms as he thought it through. "Don't forget the fact that Lionel seemed perfectly healthy earlier that evening. No signs of distress. Heart attacks can happen suddenly, sure, but..." He trailed off, leaving the thought unfinished.

Mama added "Ornaments Scattered" and "Open

Window" to the list of clues on the board. Then, after a dramatic pause, she turned and wrote "Motive?" in bold letters beneath the clues. "Who would want Lionel dead?" she mused, tapping the marker against her chin. "And more importantly, why?"

That was the million-dollar question, wasn't it? I leaned back in my chair, thinking about Lionel's life in Holiday Junction. He was beloved by most, the creator of the iconic annual Christmas ornaments. But then I remembered something—Evelyn Frost's reaction when we'd seen her at the lodge.

"Evelyn," I murmured, more to myself than anyone else.

Radley and Mama both turned to look at me.

"What about Evelyn?" Radley asked, tilting his head.

"She was upset," I said, thinking back to the exchange with Darren. "She lost out to Lionel in the ornament competition this year. And from what I gathered, it wasn't the first time."

Mama, ever quick on the uptake, scribbled "Evelyn Frost—Ornament Rivalry" on the board and circled it twice. "Jealousy is a powerful motive," she remarked, nodding in approval of her own deduction.

"It's possible, but we don't have anything solid yet," I reminded them, though I couldn't help but feel a flicker of suspicion. Evelyn had seemed... off, to say the least. "She may have been upset, but that doesn't mean she'd go as far as murder."

"We should look into it anyway," Radley said. "Better to explore every angle."

Mama wrote "Alibis" under the growing list of names and clues. "I'll bet we can find out where Evelyn was around the time Lionel died. Won't be too hard to ask around the art community. Plus, the Lodge was packed—there were plenty of witnesses."

I nodded in agreement. "Let's also think about who else might have had a reason to harm Lionel. He had been around for years—any long-standing grudges? Unresolved business deals? Maybe a falling-out with a former partner?"

Radley scratched his chin thoughtfully. "I can dig into that. I've got some old contacts from back in the day who know their way around local gossip."

"Sounds like a plan. We'll divide and conquer." Mama paused in her writing, glancing over her shoulder with a grin.

As I looked over the growing list of clues, potential motives, and names, a strange sense of excitement bubbled up inside me. We were getting somewhere. It wasn't much yet, but it was a start.

I grabbed my coffee and took a long sip, my eyes still glued to the board. "Let's stay focused, though," I said, my voice firm. "We need to keep this quiet and under the radar. The last thing we need is Jeffrey and

Annalise swooping in and making this a media frenzy."

"Agreed. We play our cards right, we'll be one step ahead of them." Radley nodded, a determined glint in his eye.

"And if we do this right," Mama said with a twinkle in her eye, "we'll solve this mystery, keep the festival going, and make sure Holiday Junction shines bright for the holidays."

I couldn't help but smile at her enthusiasm. But as I looked back at the murder board, the weight of the task ahead settled over me. Somewhere in this town, someone knew the truth about what had happened to Lionel Garland.

And it was up to us to find out who.

CHAPTER EIGHT

With plenty of things to do, we all went our separate ways but said we'd keep our eyes peeled and our ears wide open for any and all information. I told Radley I'd head over to the Christmas Lodge to gather some photos and interviews for the daily online edition. We had created a whole section in the *Junction Journal* just for the festival, and I wanted to keep it as lively and fresh as the event itself.

As I gathered my camera equipment bag, notepad, and the assortment of little things I liked to keep with me "just in case," something out of place caught my eye. Jeffrey's satchel. It sat innocently enough by the coatrack, blending in with the other items scattered around the office.

I reached for the satchel, lifting it gingerly by the

strap. It was heavier than I expected. Curiosity started to nibble at the edges of my mind.

It wouldn't hurt to take a peek, right? After all, maybe there was something in there that could give us a clue. Something about Lionel, perhaps?

He and Annalise had been digging around before everything went south, and they were interviewing Lionel as well as taking photos. It wouldn't hurt to take a look.

I bit my lip, torn between doing the right thing and letting my instincts as a reporter take over. Radley was still busy, and it didn't look like Jeffrey was rushing back anytime soon to get it.

Taking a deep breath, I gave in to temptation. My fingers worked quickly, unfastening the buckle on the satchel's worn leather flap. Inside, I found a sleek digital camera tucked away among a few notebooks and other essentials.

My pulse quickened.

What if they'd captured something during their time at the Lodge? A photo of Lionel, or perhaps some clues from their conversation with him before his untimely death? I reasoned with myself that it wasn't snooping.

It's investigative journalism.

"Yes," I whispered to myself, responding to my thoughts.

It took me all of two seconds to pull the camera

out, the weight of it solid and cool in my hands. The SD card was tucked into its side, just waiting to be accessed. I hesitated for a brief moment, my thumb hovering over the card slot.

Was this going too far?

I straightened up and looked around. No one would know. And it wasn't like I was stealing anything, right?

I was just borrowing a peek.

For the story.

For the truth.

With a deep breath, I slipped the SD card out of the camera and stared at it, turning it between my fingers as if I needed it to give me permission.

"It's not illegal," I whispered to myself, more to quell my nerves than anything else. I glanced out of my office door to the hall to make sure I didn't see or hear Mama or Radley.

I slipped the card into the desk computer then clicked through the folders, my heart pounding as I sifted through the image thumbnails. I stared at the screen, anticipation building.

With a deep breath, I clicked on the first image, the screen filling with a beautiful shot of Holiday Junction's downtown area, blanketed in soft, sparkling snow. The entire scene was straight out of a Christmas postcard. The kind of image that stirred up nostalgia and warmth all at once. In the foreground stood Mayor Paisley, the beloved Boston terrier, in her annual festive costume. This year, Kristine Whitlock, her owner and the proud proprietor of the Jubilee Inn, had her dressed as a snowman, complete with a tiny hat, coal buttons, and a bright orange carrot nose attached to her snout.

People crowded around, snapping pictures with the cheerful "Mayor," who was always a crowd favorite at the festival. Kids and adults alike grinned and posed, creating the kind of heartwarming scene that made the festival so special.

As I clicked through the images, I saw several familiar faces beaming with pride.

Jeffrey had captured the spirit of the town perfectly. Each photo felt alive with the charm and energy of the season. The downtown area was glowing, every shop window decorated with twinkling lights, garlands, and festive displays. Families wandered from stall to stall in the market, their cheeks rosy from the cold, their hands gloved as they held onto bags of Christmas trinkets or cups of hot cocoa.

"No wonder you have this nice big job at *Southern Charm*," I groaned, still clicking through the photos, knowing just how hard it was to get to their level in this job.

In one image, Santa Claus sat on a large, snow-dusted throne in front of the town's towering Christmas tree, a long line of children waiting eagerly for their turn to sit on his lap. The scene was pure magic.

The gorgeous event had been located in Celebration Park.

His photos were so vivid that I could almost hear the laughter of children filling the air. Santa's bright-red suit popped against the white of the snow, and the kids looked like little bundles of joy wrapped in their puffy coats, scarves, and mittens.

I clicked to the next image, and the screen filled with a breathtaking view of Celebration Park. Snowflakes cascaded gently from the sky to join the thick blanket of white covering the ground.

Holiday lights twinkled like stars. The scene was centered around the large fountain, which had been transformed into the crown jewel of the downtown part of the festival.

It had been turned into a massive snow globe.

The fountain's stone base had been carefully encased in a glass dome, and within, a whimsical winter wonderland had been brought to life. Tiny, glittering figures of skaters twirled on a frozen lake, their arms outstretched as they danced in sync with the rhythm of the lights overhead. A miniature Christmas tree stood at the center, its branches adorned with glittering ornaments.

Jeffrey had done a great job photographing the heart of the town. I clicked through, enjoying them so much I'd almost forgotten what my purpose for scrolling through them had been.

The photos began to move up the mountainside, where the Art District and Christmas Lodge were located. The cobblestone streets dusted with snow and the festive carriage lamps were captured by the camera. I could see the vendors' booths now, brimming with handmade crafts, ornaments, and holiday treats. Twinkling lights hung above the booths, creating a canopy of warmth through the apparent chill of the evening.

The next photo that filled the screen was breathtaking. It showed the entrance of the Christmas Lodge, the familiar stone steps blanketed in freshly fallen snow. The lodge looked magnificent. The building stood tall and proud, wooden beams and rustic stonework giving it an air of timeless grandeur. Each window was framed by the heavy snowfall, and in every one a single candle burned, illuminating the frost-coated panes. The small flames added brightness to the surrounding winter scene, enhancing the cozy warmth emanating from inside the lodge that one could almost feel just by looking at the photo.

What really caught my eye, though, were the icicles. They hung from the roof, framing the building in a delicate cascade of ice. Each icicle seemed to stretch endlessly downward, sharp and clear, clinging to the eaves and window frames like nature's own Christmas decorations. They seemed to shimmer with a frosty sheen, frozen in place by the biting cold that had settled in for the season. It was the kind of cold that would preserve these icy daggers for weeks, maybe longer, their presence making the lodge feel both inviting and just a little foreboding at the same time.

From the roofline to the tops of the lodge's grand windows, the icicles created a stunning display, some even dripping down from the bases of the lower panes. Their round edges were as smooth as glass, reflecting the light of the lodge and the snow that had continued to fall outside. It was a breathtaking yet stark contrast—the warmth and comfort radiating from inside the lodge versus the biting cold and frozen beauty that surrounded it.

Since I knew Jeffrey and Annalise had arrived at the lodge after Darren had taken me there, I figured it might be amusing to see if we'd been caught in the backgrounds of any photos—maybe a glimpse of us reflected in one of the lodge's windows, right where I knew Lionel's booth had been located. Curiosity piqued, I clicked the plus sign on the computer, zooming in on the window just for fun.

That was when something caught my eye.

It wasn't a reflection of Darren and me, as I'd half expected. Instead, it was the very same window I'd noticed cracked open earlier, but in this shot, the window was firmly closed. The detail nagged at me immediately. Why had it been cracked open later if it had clearly been shut tight when this photo was taken?

My pulse quickened. I hurriedly scanned through the rest of the photos, bypassing the charming snapshots of Lionel at his booth and the other vendors smiling brightly beside their holiday wares. I was searching for anything that showed the interior of the lodge near that window, anything that might give me more context.

But nothing.

There were no shots from inside that showed the window later in the evening. Instead, the last few images were all of the exterior of the lodge again, different angles of its snow-covered grandeur.

I almost let out a frustrated sigh—until I spotted the window again.

My heart thudded in my chest as I zoomed in on the new image. The timestamp was clearly after Jeffrey and Annalise had left the interior, meaning this shot had been taken later. The window was once again slightly ajar, but that wasn't what made my blood run cold.

The icicles.

The thick, sturdy icicles that had lined the base of

the window, impossibly hard and frozen solid when I'd first been at the lodge, were missing.

I sat back, my breath catching in my throat. The icicles that should have been dangling from the frame had been broken off—gone completely.

And I had a sinking feeling that their absence was no accident.

I gnawed on my lip and turned to look out the office window, the winter scene on the beach unfolding before me. The seaside view was stunning in its own windswept way, even in the dead of winter. The sand, usually golden and warm in the summer, was now dusted with a layer of white snow, giving it an almost surreal quality. Children bundled up in colorful coats, scarves, and hats ran along the shore, their laughter carried on the crisp ocean breeze. They kicked up the snow as they chased each other, their boots leaving a patchwork of footprints along the shoreline.

A few parents stood near the dunes, their gloved hands holding steaming cups of hot cocoa, watching their children with indulgent smiles. Beyond them, the waves crashed rhythmically against the snow-lined beach, the frothy tips curling and breaking in perfect synchronization. Gulls circled lazily above, occasionally dipping down to inspect the beach for a snack, though they seemed far less interested in the beach activity than they were in the warmer months.

I watched as one of the children bent down and shaped a snowball in his hands before tossing it at another, only to have it miss by a mile. The whole scene felt so normal, so peaceful, like something out of a holiday postcard. But my mind couldn't fully appreciate it. Not when my thoughts kept circling back to Lionel... and the mystery of his death.

I let out a long breath, my fingers tapping absently on the desk. The details of the crime scene played out in my mind again. Lionel slumped over, his body surrounded by shattered ornaments. The booth in complete disarray. But the one thing that had stuck with me—more than anything else—was the wet spot near his head.

Why had I brushed it off? A wet spot on the rug didn't seem right, especially in the middle of a cold lodge with no visible source of water nearby. There had been no signs of him hitting his head or any other injury that would explain it. And yet, that spot had been there, clear as day.

I furrowed my brow, my mind starting to piece together a troubling idea.

The window.

The icicles.

The wet spot.

A sudden, chilling thought hit me with the force of a snowstorm. What if the missing icicles weren't just some random detail? What if... they were the weapon?

I shot up in my chair, my heart thudding against my chest. My mind raced as the pieces started to click together. The window had been cracked open. Icicles had been broken off, and Lionel had a strange wet spot near his head. What if the killer had climbed through that window with one of the sharp icicles in hand? What if they had used it to stab Lionel—an icicle straight to the neck?

The image flashed through my mind, and I felt a shiver run down my spine. It would be the perfect murder weapon. There'd be no fingerprints, no blood left on the weapon... because the weapon itself would melt away. Disappearing into nothing but water.

No weapon. No evidence.

Just an empty window with a few missing icicles, and a man dead with no obvious cause.

I gasped, the realization hitting me full force.

The murder weapon had melted. But of course, it was just a theory.

CHAPTER NINE

"I'm telling you, Curtis," I said, my voice urgent as I stood across from Coroner Curtis Robinson, who was dressed in his usual blue scrubs and a well-worn lab coat, a stark contrast to the festive Christmas scene outside.

His office was located in the basement of the Holiday Junction Hospital, which was in the business district of the village, a little beyond Celebration Park.

This place gave me the heebie-jeebies and was as sterile as they came.

Clean, cold, and entirely utilitarian.

The faint hum of overhead fluorescent lights was unremitting as I glanced around the morgue. I felt the weight of the room pressing down on me as I looked for an air vent to warm myself up.

Mama had seen me standing outside of the *Junction Journal* at the trolley stop. She must've felt sorry for me because she'd come out there to give me the key to her golf cart to use for the day. She'd said she needed to walk off the extra holiday pounds she was about to put on from all the amazing cookies and candies she'd be making.

Though the golf cart was enclosed, it was so cold outside that no amount of heat generated by the cart was going to make the cab completely warm.

The morgue had an air of eerie stillness, interrupted only by the quiet ticking of a wall clock.

On one side, a metal examination table gleamed under the harsh lighting, the cold steel looking more suited for something mechanical than for a human. A few medical instruments were laid out neatly on a tray, their sharp edges glinting in the artificial light. Through the small basement window, I could see the world outside in stark contrast.

Flurries of snow drifted gently down, illuminated by strands of colorful lights decorating the nearby trees. A group of children, bundled in bright coats, laughed as they made snow angels in their front yards. The faint sound of a carol playing in the distance, which I bet was coming from the steps of the church, seemed like a mocking reminder of how vastly different things were inside.

I turned back to Curtis, who was leaning against

the counter with his arms crossed. He gave me a look that was part amusement, part exasperation. He was a no-nonsense man, rarely rattled by anything, not even a murder in the middle of a Christmas festival.

"Violet," Curtis said slowly, "why on earth are you playing detective again? You know Chief Strickland isn't exactly a fan of civilians meddling in his investigations. Especially you."

I ignored the warning in his voice. Chief Strickland and I had our past, but now that I was with Darren, I felt he had started to warm up to me.

"I have to," I replied, my tone firm. "This isn't just about me sticking my nose where it doesn't belong. It's for the good of the village, Curtis. People are already whispering about Lionel's death, and if we don't figure out what happened soon, we'll have more than just rumors to deal with. Holiday Junction doesn't need that kind of publicity. Especially during the festival. I'm trying to help."

"And how exactly do you think you can help, Violet?" He sighed, rubbing the back of his neck.

"By giving you my theory," I said, stepping closer. "Listen. Lionel didn't die of a heart attack. There's something more here, and I think I've figured it out." I swallowed hard then dove in. "I think someone used an icicle to stab Lionel in the neck."

"An icicle?" Curtis raised an eyebrow, the skepticism clear on his face, but he was clearly not surprised by the possibility that Lionel didn't die of a heart attack. "You've been watching too many crime dramas."

"I'm serious," I insisted, my voice rising. "I've been thinking about it all morning. The window at the lodge was cracked open. The icicles that were hanging there, well, some of them were missing. You said yourself that Lionel had no external injuries that would explain the wet spot by his head. I saw it once on Columbo."

"Violet…" He sighed. "Like I said, too many crime shows."

"I'm serious." There was no hint of a smile on my lips. "What did your initial autopsy find?"

Curtis's expression shifted slightly, the amusement fading into something more serious.

"Now, I'll admit, I've seen some strange things over the years, but when we got Lionel's body back to the morgue and took a closer look at that wound, I could tell something was off. At first, there was barely any visible blood, which is strange in itself with a puncture wound like his." He tapped his finger on the counter, as though marking the importance of each word. "You'd think with a wound to the carotid, there'd be a considerable amount of blood right there at the scene."

I shuddered, and he didn't miss it. He gave me a

brief, almost fatherly look of reassurance, before continuing.

"Here's the thing, Violet. Once his body began to warm up under the lights in the examination room, the wound began to bleed. Slowly, at first. Just a trickle. But it was enough to make me suspect something was suppressing it initially." He paused, the lines around his eyes deepening as he relived the realization.

"And that's when I knew to start looking at the wound a bit differently," he went on. "If your theory is right, this could explain how the cold of the icicle had temporarily slowed the blood flow plus the freezing temperatures in the room from that window, kept his body well below normal. But once he was no longer in that freezing air, his body responded as you'd expect from a puncture wound that deep."

My mind was barely able to keep up with the implications of what he was telling me.

"So you're saying the icicle itself..." My words dangled.

Colonel Holz nodded.

"Exactly. The icicle acted as a sort of... temporary dam, if you will. Its cold surface caused the blood vessels around the wound to constrict, and that's why he didn't bleed out as quickly as he might have otherwise. For a moment, anyway."

He leaned forward, his voice dropping to a confidential murmur. "I'd wager the killer knew exactly what they were doing, too. The wound was precise, not some clumsy strike. They used the icicle deliberately, knowing it would melt and disappear, leaving only the injury itself as evidence."

I let out a slow breath, trying to wrap my head around the chilling precision of the crime.

Colonel Holz straightened, crossing his arms.

"Now, Lionel's wound might have been bleeding internally even at the scene, but it was the cold of that icicle that held back the floodgates, so to speak, just long enough to make it seem almost clean. And by the time anyone found him, the weapon was already gone, melted away." Colonel had brought my theory to life.

"Plus, the wet spot at the scene. You couldn't explain it, and neither could the chief. It was the thawed icicle mixed with a little bit of blood. But if the killer used an icicle, that would explain why there was water near Lionel's body. Near his head," I said, making this more than just a theory.

Curtis let out a slow breath, his eyes narrowing as he thought through the possibilities. "I'll admit, it's a plausible theory. The cold temperatures, the window being cracked. It could explain why the crime scene didn't reveal signs of anything unusual right away," he said.

"And there's more," I said, pulling Jeffrey's camera out from my bag. "I found this in Jeffrey's satchel. He left it behind at the office, and I figured there might be something on here from his time with Lionel. They were taking photos before Lionel was found dead."

"Who is Jeffrey?" Curtis gave me a look that clearly said he wasn't thrilled about me snooping, but he didn't say anything, waiting for me to continue.

"He's with *Southern Charm*, the magazine here for the ornament winner—Lionel. I went through the photos," I said as I made sure the SD card was securely in place. "They started in the downtown area but eventually worked their way up to the lodge. When I zoomed in on one of the shots, I noticed something. The window was closed at first, icicles intact. Then, in another shot, the window is cracked open, and the icicles are missing."

Curtis moved closer, staring at the screen as I flipped through the images. His brow furrowed as he took in the evidence. "So you're saying," he murmured, his voice low, "the killer could have come through the window, used one of the icicles to stab Lionel, and then slipped back out, leaving no trace?"

"It fits, Curtis. It all fits." I nodded, feeling a surge of adrenaline.

Curtis stared at the screen for a few more moments before finally stepping back, his face unreadable. "I'll have to look into this more," he said slowly, his tone cautious. "But I can't deny that it makes sense. The wound, the water, the missing icicles... It's a stretch, but it's possible."

"So you'll tell Chief Strickland?" I asked, hopeful.

"Tell me what?" Chief Matthew Strickland's voice cut through the room, low and steady, with that unmistakable edge of authority.

He had slipped in just like the winter cold, unnoticed until he was right beside us, his presence heavy and undeniable.

Curtis straightened, tucking his hands into his pockets, while I took a small step back, suddenly feeling like a kid caught sneaking an extra cookie.

"I was just about to fill you in, Chief," Curtis said, his tone carefully neutral, but there was a flicker of unease in his eyes. "After Violet left."

"And why do I have a feeling it involves you, Violet?" Chief Strickland's gaze slid over to me, sharp as ever.

I offered a sheepish smile, trying to sound casual. "I may have stumbled across something that could help with the investigation. Curtis thinks it's plausible." I shrugged.

"Go on," the Chief said, folding his arms over his chest, his eyes narrowing with suspicion.

I took a deep breath and launched into my theory, outlining the cracked window, the missing icicles, the puncture wound on Lionel's neck, and the unexplained wet spot near his body. I could feel my heart beating a little faster as I spoke, fully aware that Chief Strickland wasn't the biggest fan of me playing detective.

When I finished, Curtis nodded in agreement.

"The theory's not as far-fetched as it sounds. An icicle could have been used as a weapon. The wound matches, and the melted ice could explain the water at the scene." He looked at Curtis to make sure this was possible. "I think I saw that on a scene in—"

"Columbo," Curtis and I chimed in together. We looked at each other and laughed.

"And I hate to say it, but I have heard that killers can get ideas from shows like that," the chief said. His face remained unreadable, but his eyes flicked toward the screen on the digital camera.

He took a step forward and held out his hand for me to give it to him.

His fingers hit the Next button of the digital camera as he clicked through the images.

"See, that one." I pointed out the photo with the open window and missing icicles.

For a moment, the room was filled with tense silence. Then, in one swift movement, Chief Strickland opened the little door of the SD card.

"I'll be taking this," he said, his tone leaving no room for argument as he slipped the SD card out of the slot. "Evidence should be in police custody, not floating around on your desk."

I opened my mouth to protest but quickly shut it. I hated to give Jeffrey back his camera without his SD card, but luckily, I'd downloaded the photos to the *Junction Journal* hard drive, which was connected to my phone, before I left the office. As a journalist, I was taught to back everything up, and I mean everything.

"Matthew," I said after a beat, choosing my words carefully, "I really think I can help here. I know this town, the people, and I've got a good sense for when something doesn't feel right. I can ask around, talk to people. Discreetly, of course. Just give me a little leeway, and I promise to report everything back to you."

He eyed me for a long moment, his jaw working as he considered my request. I could see the gears turning in his head, weighing whether it was worth letting me sniff around or better to shut me down completely.

"You want me to just let you investigate?" he finally asked, his voice thick with skepticism.

"No," I corrected quickly. "I won't investigate. I'll just keep my ear to the ground, ask a few questions here and there. Nothing too obvious. And anything I hear or see, I'll bring straight to you."

Chief Strickland's lips thinned into a straight line. I could tell he didn't like the idea of me getting involved. But then again, he knew I was stubborn and that if he outright forbade me from doing anything, I'd probably find a way to do it anyway.

He sighed, rubbing his temple with two fingers before locking eyes with mine. "All right, here's the deal," he said. "You can ask around, keep your eyes open. But"—he raised a finger—"anything you hear, anything you see, you report directly to me. No playing detective, no taking matters into your own hands. You find something, you tell me, and I handle it. Understood?"

"Understood. You've got my word." I nodded eagerly, not believing my luck.

He narrowed his eyes at me, clearly not convinced of my ability to stay out of trouble. "If I find out you're meddling, Violet, there will be consequences. I'm serious," he warned.

"I'll keep myself in line," I promised, trying to hide the small spark of victory that flickered in my chest. "I'll be your eyes and ears, nothing more."

The chief studied me for another moment before saying, "Alright then. Don't make me regret this."

He turned to leave, and Curtis shot me a wary glance. I could tell he wasn't entirely sold on the idea of me being involved either, but at least he hadn't thrown me under the bus.

"Just be careful," Curtis muttered under his breath as the chief made his way toward the door.

"I always am," I replied, giving him a wink before turning back to gather my things.

Chief Strickland paused in the doorway, glancing back at me one last time. "And Violet?" He got my attention.

"Yeah?"

"No snooping," he warned me again as if I'd not heard it the first time.

"No snooping," I repeated, my fingers crossed behind my back.

With that, he disappeared down the hallway, leaving me standing there with a mixture of excitement and trepidation. I had the chief's permission.

Sort of.

Now it was time to figure out what really happened to Lionel Garland.

And I had a strong feeling the answers were out there, just waiting to be uncovered. As the editor-in-chief of the *Junction Journal* I wasn't about to let *Southern Charm* journalists solve my own little village's big crime story.

CHAPTER TEN

The hum of Mama's golf cart was a low, steady whirl as I steered it down the snow-packed main road of Holiday Junction. A few of the buttons on the dashboard blinked, indicating that the heat was doing its best to fend off the cold air that still managed to sneak in. Mama had mentioned she had just gotten new snow tires for the golf cart, and thank goodness for that because, even though the roads were cleared and salted, there was always a fine dusting of fresh snow like powdered sugar over a cake.

Holiday Junction truly was a winter wonderland. The snow, a fluffy, thick blanket, covered every inch of the village, turning buildings into frosted gingerbread houses. Trees, strung with sparkling ornaments and bright, festive ribbons, lined the streets.

Wreaths hung from every shop door, and lampposts were draped with garlands of holly and small red-and-gold bells. Each storefront window gleamed with Christmas displays that invited shoppers to come in from the cold. Snowmen, some fully adorned with scarves and hats, others half-built and waiting for the perfect carrot nose, dotted the lawns of homes and businesses alike.

My breath fogged up the window of the enclosed cart, and I wiped the glass clear to get a better look at the people bundled in scarves and coats moving about on the sidewalks. Some clutched cups of hot cocoa from the various booths set up along the main drag, while others stood admiring the intricate window displays of toy shops, clothing boutiques, and artisan stores. The festive spirit was undeniable. Children squealed with delight as they tugged their parents toward the glowing lights of Celebration Park, where they no doubt planned to visit Santa or take a spin on the holiday carousel.

Instead of making my usual quick U-turn in the middle of the street, I decided to take the scenic route. I turned the wheel and headed toward the roundabout that ended at Celebration Park. My eyes flicked toward the entrance of the park, where snowflakes fell steadily around the fountain that had been transformed into the massive snow globe for the centerpiece of the town's winter display. Inside the globe, a charming Christmas village was recreated with miniature cottages, a carousel, and tiny figures skating on a frozen pond. The fake snow inside swirled around, mimicking the real flakes falling from the sky.

I slowed down, admiring the intricate detail of the display, which felt so real that, for a moment, I imagined stepping inside the snow globe, away from the worries and the mysteries surrounding Lionel's death. Children were gathered around the base of the snow globe, their faces lit with pure wonder as they pressed their noses to the glass, marveling at the wintry world inside.

I sighed, almost forgetting that I was on a mission until the familiar scent of freshly brewed coffee reached my nose. The kick of the smell reaching through the cold reminded me that I needed a strong cup to get through the rest of this day.

I pulled away from the park and turned onto the main street once again, my eyes landing on Brewing Beans Coffee Shop, which sat nestled between two small gift shops. It was one of my favorite places to visit, its cozy interior always offering a welcome respite from the cold. The large windows of Brewing Beans were fogged with condensation, but I could still make out the outlines of customers sitting at tables, huddled over steaming mugs. The red-and-white striped awning over the shop was dusted with snow, and a wooden sign out front boasted today's special: Peppermint Mocha Latte.

I parked the golf cart near the curb and stepped out, taking in the surrounding scene. The village was bustling with holiday shoppers and families making their way down the sidewalks. I could hear the cheerful ringing of bells, likely coming from one of the Santas stationed in front of Flowerworks who greeted passersby with a friendly wave and collected donations for the local orphanage.

Everything felt so festive, so alive with Christmas spirit, that it was hard to believe something so dark had happened just a few miles up the mountain at the Christmas Lodge. But that was exactly why I was here. To solve this puzzle, to figure out how Lionel had ended up dead amidst all this holiday cheer.

I pushed open the door to Brewing Beans, the little bell above the door jingling softly. Warmth wrapped around me like a comforting blanket as the rich, heady scent of freshly ground coffee beans filled my senses. Inside, the café was packed with people, the sound of clinking mugs and soft chatter creating a cozy hum. In one corner, a group of teens laughed loudly while playing a card game and sipping on hot chocolate. At the counter, two familiar faces greeted me with smiles—Hershal and Hazelynn Hudson, the owners, waited to take the next order.

"I told Hazelynn that you'd be here when you saw

that sign out front," Hershal said. A smile as bright as the snow outside crossed his lips.

"He sure did." Hazelynn winked and then playfully slapped his arm. "I think he made it just so you would come in."

"You know how to get me." I snickered and pointed to my heart. "I can't resist your peppermint mocha latte."

"I crushed up some extra candy canes just for you too," he said with a gesture for me to hold on before he disappeared into the back.

"Don't worry. I got your ad all ready to go live tomorrow for the big sale you're having," I assured Hazelynn. I wondered if that was the reason Hershal had made the drink special just so I'd come in.

"I'm not worried about that," Hazelynn said and slid her eyes past my shoulder. "I'm worried about her being free."

Slowly, I turned my head to see who Hazelynn was worried about.

"Evelyn Frost?" I asked after I'd turned back around. "Free?"

"Mm-hmm," Hazelynn hummed above the Christmas music piping through the coffee shop. "Come here."

She didn't waste any time. I followed her into the back, past the hustle and bustle of the front counter to the prep area where Hershal was making me a fresh baggy of the crushed-up candy canes he knew I loved. During the festive season, I liked to add them into my own personal coffee as well as keep some in my pocket for my breath.

The smells of fresh coffee, cinnamon, and chocolate mingled together, making the space feel warm and inviting. But the look on Hazelynn's face told me this wasn't just a social chat. She had something to say, and from the way she kept glancing around, she didn't want anyone else to overhear.

She leaned in closer, her voice dropping to a whisper. "I don't want to spread rumors—you know that's not my style—but Hershal and I overheard something the other day. Evelyn Frost was talking to some folks down at her shop. And what she said... well, it didn't sit right."

I raised an eyebrow, my curiosity piqued. Evelyn Frost wasn't exactly known for being mysterious, but I had seen her acting oddly lately. Especially with her reaction to *Southern Charm* being in town. "What did she say?"

Hazelynn glanced toward the door, making sure we were still alone, before she continued. "She was talking about Lionel. You know how his ornament beat hers in the competition this year? Well, she wasn't happy about it. Not one bit. I mean, everyone knows she's proud of her work, but there was something off about how she said it."

I frowned, trying to piece together what I already knew. "What exactly did she say?"

Hazelynn shifted on her feet, clearly uncomfortable repeating the words. "She said—and I swear I'm not making this up—'It should've been me. That ornament was mine. And I'll be sure no one forgets it.'"

I blinked, letting the weight of her words settle in. That didn't sound like the Evelyn Frost I knew. Sure, she was competitive and a bit of a perfectionist when it came to her work, but threatening? That was new.

"You think she meant something by that?" I asked, already knowing what Hazelynn was going to say next.

"I'm not saying she did anything," Hazelynn said quickly, holding up her hands. "But you have to admit, it's a strange thing to say right before Lionel... you know." She let the words hang in the air, knowing I didn't need her to finish the sentence.

I crossed my arms, leaning back against the counter where Hershal was busy crushing up the candy canes, blissfully unaware of the conversation happening a few feet away. My mind raced. Evelyn had always been a bit quirky, but this? This felt personal. If she truly felt like Lionel had stolen something from her, could it have pushed her over the edge?

"You think I should look into it?" I asked, my reporter instincts already gearing up for a new lead.

"I think you should be careful," Hazelynn replied, her tone serious. "Evelyn's been on edge ever since she lost the competition, and this whole thing with Lionel, well, it just feels off. If she had something to do with his death, even indirectly, I don't want you getting too close."

I nodded, appreciating her concern. But the truth was, I couldn't let this go. Evelyn Frost had suddenly moved to the top of my suspect list, and there was no way I was going to sit back and ignore what I'd just heard.

"Thanks for the heads-up, Hazelynn," I said, my mind already spinning with how I could follow this lead. "I'll be careful. Promise."

Hershal came to me at that moment with my peppermint mocha latte and a small bag of crushed candy canes in hand.

"Here you go, Violet," he said with a grin. "Extra minty, just how you like 'em."

"Thanks, Hershal. You always know how to brighten my day." I smiled, taking the bag from him and slipping it into my coat pocket.

"You're welcome, kiddo." He chuckled, oblivious to the serious conversation that had just taken place. "Now don't be a stranger."

When I walked back into the café from the back, I noticed Evelyn Frost was no longer there and that someone had already taken her table.

I made my way back through the café, my mind already working on my next move.

If Evelyn Frost had something to hide, I was going to find out. And I had a feeling the answer was waiting for me at her shop.

I stepped back outside into the winter wonderland, the festive atmosphere seeming to contrast sharply with the dark thoughts that had free rein in my head. The snow had begun to fall again, big fluffy flakes that twirled lazily in the air before settling softly on the street. I climbed into Mama's golf cart, my hands wrapped around the warm coffee cup Hershal had handed me, and tried to tuck my thoughts away for a minute, focusing on the warmth of the drink against my chilled fingers. But as I moved to start the cart, a sound caught my attention—a voice, sharp and angry, carried on the crisp winter air.

"You're as cold as ice!" A man's voice rang out, loud and heated, echoing from the alley between Brewing Beans and Emily's Treasures, a little trinket shop next door. The voice was unfamiliar to me, but the words—and the tone—made me freeze in place.

The male voice was quickly followed by a statement even more jarring. "You're as cold and hard as one of those icicles."

"Icicles?" I gasped, the word hitting me like a jolt of electricity. My eyes darted toward the alley, heart racing.

Could it be a coincidence?

Or was this somehow connected to Lionel's death?

With my curiosity piqued and my reporter's instincts kicking in, I slid out of the golf cart as quietly as possible, careful not to make any noise that might draw attention.

My steps were light as I crept toward the alley, moving along the side of Brewing Beans with its holiday wreaths hanging cheerfully on the windows. Peeking around the corner, I crouched slightly, hoping to catch a glimpse of the heated argument without being noticed.

That was when I saw them.

Standing in the narrow alley between Brewing Beans and Emily's Treasures were two figures.

Evelyn Frost and Lionel's brother, Gregory Garland.

I sucked in a breath, the shock of seeing them together sending a surge of adrenaline through me. Evelyn's face was flushed, her expression one of pure frustration, while Gregory looked equally worked up, his body tense as he gestured angrily.

"You can't just walk away from this, Evelyn," Gregory spat, his voice low but filled with fury. "You know what you did."

Evelyn's mouth set into a hard line, her eyes narrowing as she stared him down. "I did what I had to do. Don't act like you're innocent in all this," she spat.

My mind raced, trying to piece together what I was hearing.

What on earth were they talking about?

And why was Evelyn involved with Lionel's brother?

The brother who just so happened to come back to town right before Lionel died?

Was murdered.

The more I watched, the more convinced I became that this wasn't just a random confrontation. They were hiding something important.

I pressed myself closer to the building to get a better vantage point, and my foot slipped slightly on the icy ground. My heart jumped, but I managed to steady myself without making a sound. I peeked out again just in time to see Evelyn grab Gregory by the elbow, her eyes flicking nervously toward the street. For a split second, her gaze landed on me.

Panic flared in her eyes. She'd seen me.

I diverted my attention to my camera bag and quickly took it out to act as if I was taking snapshots of the festival.

Without missing a beat, Evelyn yanked Gregory toward the back of the alley. "Come on," she hissed under her breath, her voice urgent. "We need to go."

In an instant, the two of them hurried through the

alley, Evelyn practically dragging Gregory behind her as they slipped out of sight, heading in the direction of her shop.

My heart pounded in my chest, adrenaline flooding my veins.

Evelyn and Gregory, what were they up to? And what did Lionel's death have to do with it?

I stood frozen for a moment, torn between the impulse to follow them and the need to be cautious. I slid my camera back up to my eye and zeroed the lens in on them, making sure I got a few good shots just in case I needed them. Most importantly, I had proof that they were together.

As they disappeared from view, I took a deep breath, my mind buzzing with questions. I had to follow this lead, but I needed to be smart about it. From what I'd heard, Evelyn Frost wasn't the type to be easily spooked, and if she was hiding something, she'd be watching her back.

"Violet!" Emily called, her voice cheerful as ever as she waved me into her shop, Emily's Treasures.

I hesitated briefly, my mind still racing from what I had just overheard in the alleyway between Brewing Beans and her shop. But I knew I couldn't ignore her, especially not when building these kinds of relationships was crucial in a small town like Holiday Junction.

With a smile that I hoped didn't look too forced, I

waved back. Emily's shop was like a big bowl of holiday cheer, a beacon of joy in the wintery landscape of the downtown area.

The large front windows displayed a variety of glittering ornaments, festive wreaths, and racks upon racks of holiday wear. From what I could see, the shop was already bustling with customers, each of them holding some sparkly piece of jewelry or trying on an ugly Christmas sweater for the season's events.

As I stepped through the door, I was instantly wrapped in the warmth of Emily's Treasures. The scents of pumpkin spice, pine, and florals filled the air, mingling with the laughter of shoppers as they browsed through the carefully curated displays of holiday merchandise.

And Emily, wearing a bright smile and a red scarf with little jingle bells along the hem, walked behind the counter to retrieve a gaudy yet charming Christmas sweater.

Her store overflowed with all things Christmas. Baskets were piled high with ornaments, metallic garlands hung from the ceiling, and decorative stars shimmered on nearly every available surface. A large Christmas tree stood in the corner, surrounded by more baskets filled with sparkly gold and silver ornaments.

The clothing racks were bursting with festive attire including plaid skirts, sparkly leggings, and cozy holiday sweaters galore. Each piece seemed more festive than the last, with snowmen, reindeer, and Santa Claus grinning up at me from the fabrics.

The jewelry section was filled with Christmassy pieces like snowflake earrings, jingling bracelets, and necklaces with tiny holiday lights that blinked.

"This is for your mama," Emily said with the sweater in her hands. "She's going to love it! It's for the Leading Ladies' annual Christmas exchange tonight." She handed me the garment with an over-the-top combination of Christmas lights, snowflakes, and reindeer.

I held the sweater up to get a better look, the gaudy design immediately catching the attention of a few nearby shoppers, who smiled in approval. "This is… something," I said, trying to stifle a laugh. My mama would absolutely love it. Emily had even added a few extra bells and sparkly details to make sure it stood out in the exchange tonight.

"Only the best for her." Emily beamed, clearly pleased with her handiwork. "I know she likes to make an entrance, and this one will have all the Leading Ladies talking."

"That it will," I agreed, still admiring the sweater's sheer audacity. "She'll be the hit of the party."

"I've heard some interesting things around town lately. People are talking about Lionel's death, you know?" Emily's eyes sparkled with excitement, and she leaned in, her voice dropping to a conspiratorial whisper. "And not in the 'he died of a heart attack' way."

Her words made my heart skip a beat.

"I think you need to tell Darren to tell his daddy to look into Evelyn Frost." Emily wasn't just one to chat about rumors.

The fact that she was hearing whispers about Lionel, especially after what I'd overheard in the alley, set my curiosity ablaze.

"Do you think Evelyn's involved?" I asked, lowering my voice too.

Emily gave me a sly smile, her eyes darting around the room to ensure no one was eavesdropping. "I don't want to say anything for sure… but let's just say, if you're looking for someone with a motive, Evelyn might be a good place to start," she said. "And I know I'm not the only one who thinks so." She leaned in closer, her eyes gleaming with the thrill of sharing a juicy tidbit. "Let me tell you something, Violet," she whispered, glancing around once more to make sure no one was listening. "Evelyn came in here last week, just before the ornament competition, all fluffed up like one of my Christmas trees. She was on a real high horse, I tell you."

I raised an eyebrow, encouraging her to continue.

"She bought this outrageously extravagant outfit," Emily went on, her voice dripping with intrigue.

"And I mean, *extravagant*. Silver sequins, feathers, the works. She told me—told me, mind you—that she was going to win the ornament competition, and that she had already called *Southern Charm* magazine to make sure they'd be there to cover her big win."

I nearly choked on my coffee.

Emily gave a smug nod, clearly enjoying the scandalous nature of her story. "That's right. She was so confident she'd win. Practically strutted around here like she was the queen of Holiday Junction. And get this, she had the nerve to say she'd be the one bringing in all the tourists to our little town because of her 'artistic genius.'"

I couldn't help but smirk at the absurdity. Evelyn Frost, as much as I hated to admit it, had always been… well, difficult, but going so far as to invite the press before the competition results were in made her look even more ridiculous.

"Then what happened?" I asked, knowing there had to be more to this.

"Oh honey, that's the best part," Emily said, lowering her voice even further. "She came back in here today, not long before you arrived, and she returned the outfit. But it wasn't in the same condition she'd bought it in. Not even close."

My eyebrows shot up. "What do you mean?"

Emily shook her head, her mouth twisting into a knowing smile. "Oh, you've got to see it for yourself.

Come with me." She motioned for me to follow her to the back of the shop, where she kept items that had been returned.

We passed by more shelves brimming with Christmas baubles, holiday decor, and clothing racks filled with festive wear. The place was bursting with holiday cheer, but all I could think about was what could possibly have happened to Evelyn's outrageous outfit.

Emily rummaged through a pile of items and pulled out the sweater. She held it up in front of her, and my eyes went wide. It was, as she'd described, gaudy to the extreme. Silver sequins sparkled across the bodice, cascading down in intricate patterns. The sleeves had delicate, glittery feather details at the cuffs. It was designed to make a statement. A statement Evelyn Frost had intended to make at the ornament competition.

"See?" Emily pointed to the silver sequins running along the front of the sweater. "A bunch of these are missing. Just gone."

I took a closer look and saw what she meant. Several patches of the sweater were bare, the shiny sequins either torn or pulled off. I noticed that the delicate feathers on the sleeves had frayed, and a couple of them were missing altogether.

"Looks like someone had a rough night," I muttered, inspecting the damage. "Did she say what happened?"

"She didn't give me a straight answer. Just mumbled something about the evening not going as planned and handed me the sweater back with an attitude, as if it was my fault. But you know Evelyn. She can be a real pill sometimes. I didn't want the fuss, so I just let her return it. She didn't even ask for a refund, just wanted to get rid of it." Emily scoffed, crossing her arms.

"That's odd," I mused, running my fingers over the damaged fabric. "You'd think she would've kept it. I mean, with how confident she was."

Emily shrugged. "Who knows? Maybe the competition didn't go the way she thought it would. And I'm telling you, she was livid. You could see it in her eyes."

A little voice in the back of my head kept poking at me, telling me there was more to this than just a ruined outfit. Evelyn had been so sure of her win, so certain that she'd already invited the press. And now, not only had she lost, but she'd returned the outfit in shambles. I filed that information away for later, knowing it could be useful as I continued to piece things together.

"It sure is something," I sighed.

"Do you want it? I mean, it's a little damaged, but

I'm sure you could just use some thread to make sure no more sequins fall off," she offered.

"I'd love to." My tone rose as if I were so excited to wear it, but I was excited to see if I could find out what happened to it.

Evidence? Maybe Lionel's DNA on there? Did he grab for her when she stabbed him with that icicle? Oh…all the things swirled in my head.

"It's all yours," Emily said, doing a little shimmy as if a shiver just crossed over her. She dumped the outfit in a shopping bag and handed it to me.

"Do you mind if I take a couple of photos of the shop?" I asked, slipping into my usual reporter mode. "It would be great for the *Junction Journal*'s online paper, especially with the festival going on."

Emily's face lit up, her smile stretching from ear to ear.

"Oh, would you? That would be amazing! You know, I've been trying to drum up some extra business before the big rush this weekend, and a feature would help. Thank you, Violet! You've always got my back."

I grinned as I shoved the shopping bag into my camera bag and pulled out the camera to begin snapping pictures of the shop.

The warm lights, the glittering ornaments, and the festive clothes all came together to create a perfect scene of holiday cheer.

Emily fussed over a few of the displays, making sure everything was just right, while I tried to capture the merry feel of Emily's Treasures.

"Don't forget to send me the link when it goes live," Emily called as I waved goodbye and stepped back out into the snowy street.

I gave her a quick nod before I climbed back into Mama's golf cart, the smile fading from my face as the weight of what I'd learned settled in. Evelyn had a motive, that much was clear.

But questions still lingered, and none of them made sense.

Yet.

As the golf cart hummed to life, I made a mental note to follow up on that strange encounter in the alley between Evelyn and Gregory, plus the fact Evelyn took back an outfit without getting a refund. Sounded to me like there was something she was hiding, and with the outfit messed up, everything seemed to be unraveling for her.

Literally.

CHAPTER ELEVEN

"Hey, Mama," I said as soon as she answered the phone. I was steering the golf cart along the winding road toward the lodge and felt the cold biting through my gloves as I held tightly onto the steering wheel. The snow was falling more heavily now, but the roads were clear enough for Mama's cart to manage, especially since she'd gotten those big ole snow tires. "I'm on my way up to the lodge now. I made a pit stop at Brewing Beans."

"And?" she asked, her voice light and curious.

"And when I got back to the golf cart, Emily yelled for me to come in and grab your sweater for the Leading Ladies' exchange tonight," I said, shaking my head. "That saves you some time."

"Oh, good!" Mama sounded pleased. "I was going to run by there after the Leisure Center this afternoon. That Emily sure knows how to pick out a festive sweater."

I smiled, imagining the sparkling, oversized sweater Mama would love. "Yeah, you're going to love it. It's perfect for the exchange. Oh, and speaking of which, I had the pleasure of getting a little gossip while I was there," I said.

"Gossip? Do tell." Mama's interest was piqued.

"Well," I started, easing the golf cart around a gentle curve, "it seems Evelyn Frost had some big plans for the ornament competition. In anticipation of winning the competition, she splurged on an incredibly extravagant outfit from Emily's shop. Before the results were announced, she was so sure of herself that she even called *Southern Charm* magazine. She wanted them to be there to cover her big win."

I could almost hear Mama raising her eyebrows through the phone.

"Goodness gracious, before the results were even announced? Sounds like someone was counting their bells before they jingled." Mama had a way with words.

"Exactly," I agreed. "And then, of course, she didn't win, and when Lionel did, it shocked her. She even returned to Emily's Treasures today to give back the outfit, and Emily found that it was damaged. Some sequins were missing, and the feathers were frayed. Not a happy ending for Evelyn."

Mama let out a thoughtful hum. "That sounds suspicious. Evelyn's always been a bit of a… diva, but this seems extreme even for her."

"Exactly. And that's not all," I continued. "You know how there are rules in the ornament competition? What happens if the winner can't fulfill their obligations?"

"Oh yes, that's right," Mama said, her voice perking up. "The runner-up takes over. I remember because when they first introduced that rule, people made a fuss about it. They didn't want it to be all about second chances. But the village council kept it, just in case something ever happened to the winner."

"Right." I nodded, feeling a spark of realization. "So, if Lionel can't fulfill his obligation as the winner because, you know, he's dead, then the runner-up takes over."

"And Evelyn is the runner-up," Mama said, finishing my thought.

"Exactly," I said, my heart picking up speed. "It all lines up. She thought she was going to win, but when Lionel took the prize, she realized the only way she could get the recognition she craved was if he… wasn't around anymore."

Mama let out a low whistle. "That's a pretty powerful motive," she sang out. "I don't know Evelyn, but that sure gives her a reason to do something drastic."

"Yeah," I agreed, my mind racing with possibilities. "And think about it. If she had already invited *Southern Charm* to cover the festival and her big win, she couldn't back out when she lost. She had to make sure she still got the attention."

Mama was silent for a moment, the sound of her thoughtful breathing coming through the phone. "You might be onto something, Violet. But let's not forget, motives don't make someone guilty. We've still got to figure out if she had the means and opportunity." Mama had a way of bringing me off the high of thinking I'd solved it.

"I know," I said, biting my lip as I drove. "Something's not right with her. I saw her having a heated conversation with Gregory Garland outside of Brewing Beans earlier today. They seemed like they were arguing about something, and when I approached, she grabbed him and hurried off."

"Gregory?" Mama asked, surprised. "What do you think they were talking about?"

"I don't know," I admitted, frustrated that I hadn't been able to hear more. "But it wasn't a friendly chat, that's for sure."

I drove the golf cart through the quaint art district, and the familiar charm of Holiday Junction seemed even more magical under the dusting of fresh snow.

Every shop window displayed Christmas decorations, ranging from hand-painted ornaments to carved nativity scenes. Christmas lights hung on every storefront, creating a canopy of shimmering color above the narrow streets.

I passed my apartment building and couldn't stop myself from glancing up to my balcony where the window boxes hung. A tiny Christmas tree was nestled in each one, and their branches had battery-operated colored lights that twinkled against the snowy backdrop.

The cheerful display was so cute and added that splash of holiday spirit I'd wanted for my apartment. It was those window boxes that had made me love the place before I'd even walked through the door.

I smiled, thinking of how cozy it would be to return there later and curl up with a mug of hot cocoa by the fireplace. Of course, with Darren by my side.

Farther along, the bustling Christmas Market came into view.

It was one of my favorite spots during the holidays, and today was no exception. Despite the cold, the market was alive with the cheerful buzz of shoppers and vendors. Stalls lined both sides of the street, offering everything from handmade crafts to steaming cups of cider. Children with bright-red noses who were bundled in layers of scarves and hats squealed with delight as they tugged their parents toward the wooden stalls filled with toys and festive treats.

The scent of roasted chestnuts wafted through the air, mingling with the crisp scent of pine and the sweetness of cinnamon from the nearby baker's stall. A large decorated Christmas tree stood in the center of the market, its branches laden with shimmering ornaments and silver garlands. The tree topper, a sparkling star, glinted in the late afternoon light, drawing everyone's eyes toward its brilliance.

I slowly weaved through the market traffic, being careful not to disrupt the magic unfolding around me as I headed toward the narrow road that led to the lodge.

As I drove past the hustle and bustle of the market, the road wound upward, and I noticed Evelyn Frost standing in front of the Jingle & Mingle shop, sipping on a steaming cup of cocoa while talking with the Blackwell sisters.

The Blackwell sisters, Betty, Beatrice, and Belle, were the village's quintessential trio of charm and mystery.

They had moved to Holiday Junction only a few years ago, taking over the Jingle & Mingle shop, a quaint little boutique that specialized in handmade holiday ornaments, artisanal gifts, and a treasure trove of festive delights. I had gotten to know them well, especially after they placed an ad in the *Junction Journal* last year for their seasonal Christmas Around the World event.

Their feature had been a hit, drawing in tourists from all over to purchase traditional holiday crafts and sweets from different cultures.

Betty, the eldest, was always impeccably dressed in vintage-inspired clothes, her salt-and-pepper hair styled into a neat bun. She had a no-nonsense attitude but a soft spot for the town's gossip, making her both feared and adored by the locals. Beatrice, the middle sister, was more soft-spoken, often handling the creative side of the business. She had an eye for design, and her handmade wreaths and garlands were always the first to sell out. Belle, the youngest, was the most outgoing of the three. With her wild red curls and constant chatter, she was the life of any event and could charm anyone into buying one of their signature ornaments.

As I drove past, I noticed Evelyn holding court with the sisters, clutching her steaming mug while Belle's enthusiastic laughter floated through the crisp air. Whatever they were discussing seemed animated, Evelyn gesturing with one hand as she spoke. Betty, always the observant one, caught my gaze and offered me a knowing smile, her sharp eyes twinkling with amusement.

I couldn't help but wonder what Evelyn was doing there mingling with the Blackwell sisters. I filed the thought away, making a mental note to ask them about Evelyn when I checked in with them about their ad for the *Junction Journal* before meeting Mama for lunch.

I guided the golf cart up the road to the lodge, which wasn't too far away.

My thoughts snapped back to my conversation with Mama, who was still on the line. "I'm pulling up to the lodge now, but I wanted to run all of this by you. Evelyn has a motive, and her behavior has been suspicious, but I still need to piece it all together. Maybe I can dig up more while I'm here," I told Mama.

"Be careful, Violet," Mama warned gently. "This is sounding like more than just small-town gossip. If Evelyn really is involved in something dangerous, you don't want to be caught in the middle."

"I know, Mama," I reassured her. "I'll keep my eyes open and my head on straight. But I've got a feeling that Evelyn isn't the only one with something to hide."

"Call me later, and we can grab lunch at Freedom Diner if you've got time," Mama said, her tone lighter now. "The daily special is turkey pot pie, and you know Nate makes the best."

"Deal," I said, laughing softly. "I'll call you once I'm done here."

I hung up the phone as I parked the golf cart in front of the lodge, my mind already buzzing with theories.

I stepped out of the golf cart, and snow crunched beneath my boots as I made my way toward the lodge. The grandeur of the building never failed to amaze me. But this morning, my focus wasn't on the festive beauty of the lodge. My eyes were drawn to the windows, specifically the one I'd found cracked open last night when I'd found Lionel.

I stopped just short of the entrance and let my gaze wander over the building to trace the snow-covered sills and sparkling icicles that hung from the eaves like nature's ornaments. The window that had been slightly ajar the night of Lionel's death was closed now.

I took a deep breath, narrowing my eyes.

Pulling out my phone, I scrolled through the photos of Jeffrey's that I'd downloaded to the server at the *Junction Journal*.

He'd captured every angle of the lodge in all its festive glory. My thumb hovered over the picture of the lodge's front from the night of the event. I swiped through a few more, pausing when I came across a shot that had been taken earlier in the evening.

I zoomed in on the window in question and thought about the theory I had given Curtis and Chief Strickland.

The icicles hanging from the ledge were long and sharp, reflecting the amber light from the Christmas lights decorating the outdoor Christmas Market.

They gleamed in perfect formation, hanging straight down in rows like frozen daggers.

I glanced up from my phone and back at the lodge, focusing on that same window. My breath caught in my throat.

Even though I knew from the photo that the icicles were gone, it was another thing to see it in person, bolstering that gut feeling that I was right.

Frowning, I toggled my gaze between the photo and the actual window several times, my heart beating faster with each pass. The first photo Jeffrey took definitely showed all the icicles attached to the window, and in the second one he took, which had a timestamp from later in the evening, the icicles were gone.

The icicles on the other windows hadn't melted away. There was no way that could have happened with the temperatures way below freezing.

They were all intact, hanging exactly as they had been, glistening in the evening glow. But on that one window, the icicles were missing.

All of them.

Taken all together, it did make sense. The wet spot near Lionel's head—near his neck—was not blood, so it was very plausible that an icicle was the murder weapon.

Plus, Coroner Curtis Robinson had found a stab wound near the carotid artery that hadn't made sense to anyone at first. The shape of the wound didn't align with that of any weapon the paramedics or investigators had considered.

This theory explained everything—the open window, the scattered ornaments, and the wet spot by Lionel's head.

CHAPTER TWELVE

I slipped my phone back into my coat pocket, my fingers still trembling with a mix of cold and the weight of my discovery. The thought of those missing icicles and the cracked window gnawed at me as I turned away from the lodge and looked down the mountainside.

I'd already thought I was on the trail to discovery with my loosely formed and strange theory of the icicle, but even Chief Strickland confirmed as much when he agreed it was possible.

The snow had begun to fall even more heavily now, thick flakes swirling through the air and coating everything in a soft white blanket. The roads would be getting slick soon, meaning my drive back into the village in the golf cart would be slow and treacherous. I pulled my coat tighter around me, shivering not just from the cold but from the unsettling realization that the truth about Lionel's death might be more sinister than anyone suspected.

I turned back to the lodge. Remembering the cozy atmosphere before Lionel died, I made the quick decision to go inside. There was no use trying to leave now, at least not until I'd done a little more digging.

Inside, the crackling fire in the stone hearth, the soft murmur of conversation, and the twinkling Christmas decorations made me feel worlds away from the dark thoughts that had occupied my mind. I shook off the snow from my coat and glanced around.

Jessica was at the front desk, her head bent as she scribbled something into the guest register.

I wondered if she knew more than she was letting on. She'd been here, and she had to have noticed something.

I walked over, keeping my tone casual as I spoke. "Hey, Jessica." I gave her a smile.

She glanced up, offering a polite but strained smile. "Oh, Violet. Anything new with what happened to Lionel?" she asked in a lower tone, as though she didn't want any of the guests or festival-goers there for the inside market to overhear as they milled around us.

"Just trying to piece a few things together," I said, leaning casually on the counter. "It's still hard to believe." I kept my voice light but watched her carefully.

Her fingers twitched slightly as she closed the register. "It's awful," she agreed, her voice low. "He was such a big presence around here the last few weeks that it feels empty without him."

"I was wondering if you could help me out. I'm trying to get a better understanding of what happened that night. Things like who was around, what people saw, that kind of thing," I said.

She hesitated for a moment, her eyes darting around the lobby before landing back on me. "Yeah, I was here, and you saw me," she said. Though, technically, I hadn't seen her before I found Lionel. I'd just heard the movie playing in the room behind the counter.

"Did you notice anything unusual that night? That day? Maybe before I found Lionel?" I asked, keeping my tone gentle.

Jessica shifted uncomfortably and glanced toward the large windows, her fingers fiddling with the pen in her hand. "I mean, there were people coming and going for the market. The lodge was busy. Earlier that night, before you and Darren arrived, Lionel was kind of particular about how he wanted his booth set up," she said. This was a little tidbit of information that she might not have thought was important but that could have proven to be very significant to me.

I raised an eyebrow. "Particular?" I asked, hoping to get more out of her.

"More like... controlling." She let out a nervous laugh. "He wanted his display in a very specific spot near the windows, but there was a bit of back-and-forth about it."

"Back-and-forth?" I pressed gently.

"Well, I wouldn't call it an argument, but..." Jessica hesitated. "He and I had a little disagreement about the placement of his booth. He wanted to move it at the last minute, even though we'd already assigned spaces for the vendors. I told him we couldn't make changes at that point, but Lionel, well, he wasn't someone you could say no to easily."

I could see the discomfort on her face.

"Did anyone else overhear this?" I asked.

"I'm not sure," she admitted, her eyes flicking toward the hallway that led to the event rooms. "Some of the staff might have. Maybe a few of the other vendors. It wasn't a huge scene, but it wasn't exactly quiet either."

Interesting. Lionel had been arguing with Jessica about something as simple as his booth placement. *Could there have been more to it?*

"Do you know if anyone else had issues with Lionel that night?" I asked, trying to dig a little deeper.

"Well, there was some tension, I think. Especially with the whole ornament competition. People were... let's just say, not thrilled that he'd won again." Jessica looked thoughtful for a moment.

"Like who?" I asked, leaning in a little more.

"I didn't hear any specifics, but there was some whispering going around. Lionel wasn't the most well-liked person, especially among some of the other artists. He had a bit of an ego." She shrugged slightly.

I filed that away in my mental list of motives. Competition could easily push someone over the edge, especially when it involved pride, reputation, and holiday prestige.

"Thanks, Jessica. That helps." I gave her a small smile, trying to keep the atmosphere light even though my mind was racing with new possibilities. "Please, if you remember anything, let me or Darren know."

"About that..." She hesitated, her eyes turning glossy like she was about to cry. "I know you heard the Christmas movie on, so please don't tell Darren. I'll get fired for not watching the counter, especially now that this has happened."

"Oh, Jessica," I whispered and held out my hands to try to comfort her.

"If I hadn't been back there"—her voice cracked, and a tear fell—"the killer mightn't've gotten past me, or at least I'd have seen someone. Lionel might be still alive."

"Jessica." I tsked. "You cannot take that on. You didn't cause what happened to Lionel. Besides, I don't think the killer came through that front door."

Jessica wiped her tears from her cheeks and shook her head, confused.

"Last night, I noticed the window near Lionel's booth was cracked open," I started to tell her.

"How? I know we all checked them per Darren's instructions yesterday because it's so cold out," she said with a startled tone. "Please don't write an article on this. Darren has worked so hard for this to open smoothly."

"I'm not," I said, leaving the "yet" off the end. "I'm trying to help Chief Strickland out with the investigation."

"So you won't mention the Christmas movie to Darren?" she asked.

I lifted my finger to my lips and did the "zip" gesture.

"I'm not so sure his dad won't though," Jessica said, her face clouded over. "He was here a little bit ago, looking around outside and at the window. Asking all sorts of questions. Like you."

"He was?" I asked, glad to know that my little theory about the weapon and how Lionel was killed was definitely on the chief's radar.

I was kinda proud of myself.

I turned away from the desk and glanced around the lobby. There were a few guests lounging by the fire, their conversations soft and cheerful as they sipped hot cocoa and mulled cider. Most seemed blissfully unaware of the dark cloud that hung over the lodge.

I needed to talk to more people. The staff, especially. Someone must have seen something or heard something. My mind raced with possibilities. Evelyn had a motive, that much was clear, but there were still gaps in the story, and Lionel's disagreement with Jessica over the booth placement felt like a piece of a larger puzzle.

For the next twenty minutes or so, I walked around the inside market, asking the vendors if they'd seen anything or heard rumblings yesterday or even during the last few weeks as they'd set up their booths, but none of them had. They'd all been too busy with their own booths and getting them ready for the grand opening.

I even took out my phone to compare the photos Jeffrey had taken during the festivities before Lionel's death to the real-life happenings surrounding me.

I made my way toward the hallway leading to the back of the lodge, where some of the staff were gathered.

I overheard a few hushed voices coming from around the corner and paused.

"That was quite the scene last night," one of the voices said, barely above a whisper. "I've never seen Lionel that worked up before."

"Yeah," another voice replied. "I thought Jessica was going to lose it when he kept insisting on moving his display. He wasn't taking no for an answer."

I edged closer, careful not to be seen as I listened in.

"Well, whatever happened, it didn't end well for him, did it?" the first voice added ominously.

I stepped closer, trying to appear casual despite the flutter of nerves in my stomach. The two staff members, both young, probably in their early twenties, gave me wary glances but didn't stop me as I approached.

"Sorry to interrupt," I said, keeping my voice friendly. "I'm just trying to piece together what happened the other night with Lionel. You mentioned he was pretty worked up. Anything you can share could help."

They exchanged another glance. One of them, a girl with curly brown hair tucked into a wool beanie, spoke up first. Her name tag read Rabina.

"Yeah, it was... weird. I mean, Lionel could be difficult sometimes, but that night he was on edge. And then there was the whole thing with Jessica."

"What about Jessica?" I asked, keeping my tone light.

The second staff member, a guy wearing an oversized lodge sweatshirt with an employee name tag that read Josh, chimed in. "They had words over where his booth should be. Lionel was pushing to move it, but we'd already assigned the spaces. Jessica was getting frustrated, but she kept it professional, you know? Tried to stay calm, but Lionel wasn't having it."

"And what happened after that?" I pressed.

"He eventually backed off. But he wasn't happy. Jessica looked ready to pull her hair out by the end of it." Rabina shrugged.

I nodded, sensing there was more. "Anything else? Did anyone else have issues with Lionel that night?"

Josh shifted on his feet and gave a sheepish look. "Well, there was this other guy. Older, kinda rough around the edges. He came storming in, tracking snow everywhere. He was... intense."

"Yeah, super rude. He had those big, muddy boots, and we had just cleaned the floors. He stomped all over them like he didn't care." Rabina grimaced.

"Who was he?" I asked, my interest piqued. "What was he doing here?"

"We didn't catch his name." Josh scratched the back of his head. "He came in all flustered, like he was looking for someone. Turned out it was Lionel.

When he found him, they started talking, but it wasn't a pleasant conversation. The guy was sweating like crazy, like he'd just run a marathon in the snow."

"Yeah, he was all over the place. Kept fidgeting, wiping his forehead. At one point, he tried to open one of the windows." Rabina nodded.

My heart skipped a beat.

"Open the window?" I asked as if I hadn't heard her correctly.

"Yeah," Rabina said. "One of us had to go over and tell him not to. I mean, it was freezing outside, and we didn't want to mess up the temperature inside for the vendors and guests. Plus, our boss asked us to keep the windows closed. But that guy, he acted all defensive about it. Said he needed fresh air or something."

"He was jittery," Josh chimed in again. "Kept looking around like he was paranoid. And he didn't stay long. He left pretty soon after talking to Lionel."

A knot formed in my stomach. "Do you remember what time this was?"

Josh frowned, thinking for a moment. "Maybe an hour or so before everything went down between Lionel and Jessica," he said. "He stormed out not long after trying to open that window."

My mind was racing then, connecting the dots. The man, whoever he was, seemed desperate, sweating, anxious, and fixated on the window. And if he had been trying to open the very window near where Lionel was found, it was starting to feel like more than a coincidence.

"Did Lionel seem upset after their conversation?" I asked, trying to get more.

"He didn't look happy. But Lionel was always a bit grumpy, you know? I just figured it was one of his typical moods." Rabina shrugged.

"Do you remember anything else about the man? What he looked like?" I asked, my pulse quickening.

Josh shook his head. "Not really. He was tall, maybe late fifties or sixties, grayish hair. Looked like he didn't belong here, if you know what I mean. Not someone you'd expect at a Christmas festival," he said.

"Okay, thanks. You've both been really helpful," I said, managing a smile as I processed the information. "If you think of anything else, let me know."

I put my hand in my bag and took out a card. I could see the expression on their faces when they read it.

"Wait, you're not with the police?" He waved his hands in front and took a step back. "I'm sorry. I'm not talking to any reporters, especially after those other two were here," Josh said.

"Other two?" I asked.

"Here." Rabina pulled out a business card to show me.

I took it and saw it was Jeffrey's card from *Southern Charm* magazine.

"What was he asking about?" I was curious.

The two exchanged a glance.

Rabina hesitated before speaking again. "They were mostly asking about Lionel. Wanted to know all about the ornament competition, how Lionel got chosen, and if there was any drama with the other contestants," she said.

I raised an eyebrow, my pulse quickening.

"What kind of drama?" I wanted to know all the details, even if I'd heard them before. Everyone had a different perspective, and you never knew when someone would notice something important.

Josh, still looking a bit nervous, shifted on his feet. "I mean, you know how it is with these contests. There's always someone who feels like they should have won. The reporters asked if Lionel had any enemies or if anyone seemed upset about him winning. But honestly, who wouldn't be? He wins every year, and that kind of ruffles feathers." Josh shrugged.

"Yeah, they were really interested in if anyone might've held a grudge against Lionel. But they were pushy about it, asking if anyone had argued with him or seemed 'off' that night," Rabina said in agreement.

I clenched my jaw. Jeffrey and Annalise were digging around, trying to find dirt on the same people I was. But there was a key difference.

They were outsiders.

They didn't know Holiday Junction like I did. They didn't know the people, the history, or the nuances of this town's dynamics.

The last thing I needed was some out-of-town journalists swooping in and solving the murder before me.

That wouldn't just be bad for the town.

It'd be a disaster for my career.

If they cracked this case before I did, I'd never live it down. And worse, my reputation as the editor-in-chief of the *Junction Journal* would take a hit.

I took a deep breath, forcing a smile despite the frustration building inside me. "Thanks for the info. If you remember anything else, let me know, okay?" I wanted a confirmation.

Rabina nodded, still looking a bit nervous. "Sure thing." She looked at Josh. "At least you're local. And we did see you with our boss."

Ahem. I cleared my throat, trying to remain in the journalistic frame of mind and push out thoughts of the most romantic night of my life. Well, before someone was murdered.

"If they come back around, or if you think of anything else, don't hesitate to reach out. And trust me, I'm here to help sort this out, not blow it up like they might," I confirmed just as something dawned on me. "Can I ask you one more question?"

"Sure," they both said and nodded.

"I'm going to show you a photo. If you don't mind, can you tell me if you see anything off?" I took out my phone and swiped through things to bring up the photos from Jeffrey's files, continuing until I got to the one with Lionel in it.

I handed them the phone. Rabina used her fingers to pinch out the photo, and she pulled the phone closer.

"That's the guy," she said. "The guy that was causing all the ruckus."

"Lionel?" I asked as I walked closer to look from just behind her right shoulder.

"No, the guy right there, holding the ornament at Lionel's booth." She made the photo even bigger.

"Yeah. That sure is," Josh confirmed.

"Are you sure?" I asked, knowing it was Gregory Garland, Lionel's brother.

Or should I say, the long-lost brother Darren had told me about.

"Yep. I'm positive," she said and nodded. "When someone makes a fuss, especially during such a festive time and event, you notice."

"Thank you," I gushed with excitement. "Thank you."

My mind was already racing.

If Jeffrey and Annalise were asking about the

same suspects, it meant they were on to something. Or at least, they thought they were.

I knew I had to move faster. Not just for the sake of the investigation, but for my own career. If I could solve this case before them, I'd not only protect the town from their prying eyes but also prove to myself and everyone else that I was more than capable of handling this big story.

A *real* story.

CHAPTER THIRTEEN

I didn't leave the area, as I knew I needed to see the Blackwell sisters and follow up with them about their ad. Plus, Mama had told me this morning they'd left a few messages for me to call them.

With me seeing Evelyn there a little bit ago, I knew she was in the area, and if I could question her while I was there, it would be perfect.

Of course, I planned to heed Chief Strickland's stern advice to not snoop, but taking photos for the *Junction Journal* was already on my to-do list, so I walked through the outdoor Christmas Market with my camera in hand, eyes wide as I took in the scene.

It was like I had walked straight into the North Pole where Santa lives.

Wooden booths, draped in pine garlands and red ribbons, lined the cobblestone path. The air was filled with the comforting scents of cinnamon, roasted chestnuts, and hot chocolate. Snow fell softly now, large flakes sticking to the evergreen boughs that decorated each vendor stall. Twinkling lights, multi-colored and delicate, wrapped around lampposts and draped across awnings, making the entire space feel magical.

Families milled about, their laughter blending with the sounds of a Christmas carol drifting from a small band playing near the entrance. Children bundled in bright scarves and hats giggled as they sipped cocoa from oversized mugs. Booths overflowed with hand-carved wooden toys, glittering ornaments, and festive wreaths. Despite the chill in the air, the whole market exuded a cozy, inviting warmth.

One booth in particular caught my eye. It was filled with handmade ornaments crafted from silver and glass. They shimmered under the market lights, reflecting the bright snow. I raised my camera and snapped a few shots of the delicate decorations. Then the soft jingling of sleigh bells nearby drew my attention to a vendor selling rustic holiday decor.

I moved slowly through the crowd, pausing every so often to capture the essence of the holiday market. Each booth had its own unique charm. Some were packed with whimsical trinkets, while others showcased luxurious scarves, mittens, and artisanal chocolates. One booth sold hot roasted chestnuts, their sweet nutty scent wafting through the air. The vendor, wearing a woolen hat, smiled warmly as he handed out steaming paper cones of the chestnuts to waiting customers.

In the center of the market stood the giant Christmas tree, towering over everything with its oversized ornaments, silver tinsel wrapped around its branches, and a glowing star perched at the top. It was a perfect holiday scene, one that belonged on the front of a greeting card.

I adjusted my coat and the scarf around my neck as I made my way through the snowy market, passing booth after booth of holiday goodies. My fingers were practically frozen to my camera at this point, but I wasn't going to let a little cold keep me from capturing the perfect festive photos for the *Junction Journal's* holiday edition.

Or a killer.

My next stop was the Blackwell sisters' booth.

"Violet! There you are!" Belle, the youngest of the Blackwell sisters, called out as she spotted me approaching. She waved frantically, the reindeer on her thick holiday sweater bouncing along with her red curls she moved. "We were just saying we hoped you'd stop by."

"I told her you'd come by today, didn't I?" Betty, the oldest of the sisters, chimed in, not even waiting for me to respond before continuing, "Oh, she's so busy, though! Did you hear about the big scoop with Lionel? Such a tragedy." Her words were fast and overlapped with Belle's.

Beatrice, the middle sister, cut in, her voice louder to get attention, "And we've been waiting to hear back about that ad we left with you. Millie Kay said you'd get us into the paper." Beatrice always had this air of importance, like she was managing a business empire instead of a booth stacked with garlands and tree ornaments.

I smiled, unable to help myself, as the three sisters' voices tangled into one amusing, slightly confusing conversation. Betty was dressed in a festive red-and-green plaid dress with her white hair pulled into a bun that looked ready to topple at any moment. Beatrice, in a fur-lined coat, had on what looked like Santa earrings that jingled when she turned her head. Belle, as always, was the most colorful.

"Yes, yes, I got your messages," I said, trying to get a word in edgewise. "That's actually why I stopped by."

"I told you, sisters, Violet doesn't forget her old friends, especially not during the holidays," Betty said.

"Oh, of course she doesn't. How could she?" Belle jumped in, grinning ear to ear. "Did you see the giant peppermint wreath I made? Oh, Violet, it's perfect for the *Journal*'s feature on festive trends."

I opened my mouth to respond, but before I could get a word out, Beatrice was already leaning in, nudging me slightly. "And you must check out our gingerbread-scented candles. Just the thing to add a little magic to your readers' homes."

"Ladies, I promise I'm getting to all of that." I smiled warmly, pulling my camera from my bag. "But first, I need to ask you a couple of quick questions. I've been working on Lionel's story—"

"Such a terrible loss," Belle cut in, shaking her head sadly. "You know, we were just telling Evelyn here that Lionel had a bit of a temper on him, especially when things didn't go his way."

I raised an eyebrow at Evelyn, who had been watching the exchange quietly, her gaze sharp. "Oh? Did he have an issue here at the market?"

Evelyn smiled politely, but there was a subtle tension behind it. "Lionel was... competitive," she said, her tone measured. "He didn't like being told no. But then, you probably know that by now."

I couldn't miss the way Evelyn carefully avoided giving any details. She was good at this, too good. But I wasn't about to let her off the hook. "I've been hearing that Lionel was more worked up than usual the night he died. Were you two in contact much that evening?"

"Oh, we chatted briefly, but nothing out of the ordinary. You know how these markets can be—so busy it's hard to keep track of everyone." Evelyn's smile didn't falter, but her grip on her cocoa cup tightened ever so slightly.

Betty, always the most oblivious to tension, jumped in again. "Oh, Violet, you should have seen the man who came in before Lionel started acting all huffy. Tracked snow all over the place with those awful boots. So rude! He went right up to Lionel and started going on about something. I didn't catch what, though."

"Really?" I asked, curiosity piqued. "Do you remember what he looked like?"

"Oh, honey, how could I forget?" Beatrice chimed in. "Tall, older man, grayish hair, looked like he hadn't shaved in a week. He was sweating like he was running a race, and we were inside. Ridiculous, I tell you. And to make matters worse, he kept fidgeting, trying to open the window nearest Lionel's booth."

A chill ran down my spine. The window. The one I had seen cracked open after Lionel's death.

I kept my face neutral, but inside, my mind was racing. "What happened after that?" I asked, trying to sound casual.

"Oh, well, one of us had to tell him to leave the window alone, of course," Belle said, rolling her eyes. "It's freezing outside. We didn't want everyone catching colds."

"And then he left shortly after," Betty added.

"Didn't say much, just stomped out the door. Lionel didn't seem too pleased, though."

I glanced at Evelyn again, but she was focused on her cup, not meeting my gaze. Something about this didn't sit right. Why hadn't Evelyn mentioned any of this earlier?

"Well, thank you for the information," I said, slipping into a more businesslike tone. "And about the ad for the *Junction Journal*—I'll be sure to feature your booth in the holiday spread. Those peppermint wreaths will be a hit."

"Oh, wonderful," all three sisters exclaimed at once, nearly bouncing with excitement.

As I snapped a few photos of their booth, I wondered if Evelyn was telling me everything. And with this new bit of information about the man trying to open the window, my instincts were screaming that I was getting closer to uncovering the truth.

"I must hurry to catch the trolley back to the village," Evelyn said, her voice cool and controlled. I saw it as the perfect opportunity to get her alone.

"I'm going to the village now too. I have plenty of time to meet Mama for lunch," I said, turning to her with a friendly smile. "I've got Mama's golf cart. Wanna ride?"

Evelyn's eyes flickered with hesitation as she glanced outside at the heavy snowfall. "Not in this weather on these roads," she replied, pointing to the thick snow layering the ground.

"Mama's got snow tires on that thing," I said with confidence, pulling out all the stops so she couldn't refuse. "And if we leave now, we'll be just fine. Plus, it's enclosed, with heat."

Evelyn hesitated, pursing her lips. I could almost see the wheels turning in her mind, trying to figure a way out of it. But after a moment, she gave a curt nod.

"Alright, but only because I don't want to wait for the trolley in this weather." She shook her head.

I grinned, pretending this was a friendly ride back to the village when in reality I had a whole list of questions burning a hole in my pocket. She might have thought she could keep a tight lip in public, but in the cozy confines of Mama's golf cart, she wouldn't have anywhere to hide.

Once we were both settled inside the cart, I started driving carefully along the snowy road that led down the mountain. The tires crunched over the thick layer of snow as the windshield wipers cleared the falling flakes.

I glanced at Evelyn out of the corner of my eye. She was staring straight ahead, her cocoa cup clasped tightly in her hands, her knuckles pale.

"So, I overheard something interesting earlier," I began casually, gripping the wheel with one hand as I tried to ease into the conversation. "Someone said they heard you mention, 'That ornament was mine, and I'll be sure no one forgets it' when it came to you not winning. That's pretty passionate, wouldn't you say?"

Evelyn's eyes narrowed slightly, her lips tightening. "That's hardly anyone's business, is it?" she replied, her voice sharp.

"True, true," I said, playing it cool as I navigated a particularly slippery patch of road. "But with Lionel winning the competition, I just wondered if there were rules for situations like that. You know, what happens if the winner can't fulfill their obligations?"

I saw Evelyn stiffen beside me, her posture going rigid. She remained silent for a moment before speaking, her voice clipped. "The runner-up takes over, of course."

"Ahh, that's what I thought. Which would make you the runner-up, wouldn't it?" I asked, my tone light, though I could feel the tension rising in the small space. "Pretty important role, being the next in line if something happens."

Evelyn didn't respond, but her eyes were focused ahead, her fingers drumming against the cup.

"Oh, by the way," I added nonchalantly, "I stopped by Emily's Treasures earlier. She mentioned you returned that extravagant outfit you bought, but there was something strange about it."

"Strange?" Evelyn's head snapped toward me, her eyes narrowing. "What do you mean by that?"

I glanced at her for a second before digging into my bag, still keeping one hand on the wheel. "Well, Emily said some of the silver sequins were missing. I thought maybe you'd want to check it out." I fumbled, trying to pull the outfit from my bag while keeping one eye on the snowy road.

Evelyn's eyes widened as I took my hand off the wheel to rummage through my things, and she reached out, her voice tight with panic. "Violet, watch the road!"

I shrugged, not stopping my rummaging.

"It's fine. Mama's cart practically drives itself. Anyway, here's the outfit, see the missing sequins?" I finally pulled the garment free, holding it up with one hand as I nearly missed a patch of ice.

Evelyn's eyes darted from the road to the outfit then back to me. "Violet, for heaven's sake, will you please keep both hands on the wheel?" she snapped, her voice cracking.

"Fine, fine," I said, dropping the outfit back into my bag and grabbing the steering wheel with both hands again. Evelyn was pale now, and I figured I had her on the edge of breaking. "But seriously, why'd you return the outfit? Seems like it was perfect for the festival unless you crawled through a window with an icicle in your grip and the sequins snagged."

Evelyn swallowed hard, her gaze fixed straight ahead. "I didn't need it after all. That's all," she blurted.

"Or maybe it was because Lionel won, and you didn't?" I asked, pressing gently but relentlessly. "And used said icicle to stab him, leaving no weapon behind when it melted?"

Evelyn's hand clenched around her purse, and for a moment, I thought she might snap. But then she let out a long breath and said, "I left the market that night before anything happened. I went to the old theater for the midnight screening of *It's a Wonderful Life*. I have the ticket in my purse if you want proof."

I glanced at her purse. She fumbled with it, pulling out a crumpled movie ticket, her hand trembling slightly as she offered it to me.

I took the ticket, glancing at it briefly. Sure enough, it was for the midnight show, the same night Lionel was killed.

"Well," I said, handing the ticket back, "I guess that gives you a pretty solid alibi."

"Yes, it does. Keep it." Evelyn exhaled, her tension finally breaking. "And if you think I'd throw everything away over some ornament competition, Violet, you're more naïve than I thought."

I smiled faintly, pulling into the village just as the snow began to pick up again.

"Thanks for the ride," Evelyn muttered as she climbed out of the golf cart.

"Don't mention it," I said.

"And just so you know, I declined the prize for the winning ornament. Evelyn Frost is not going to win by default. So they are giving the prize to Lionel's next of kin," she said before she walked away.

I had my answers, for now. Evelyn might have an alibi, but that didn't mean I was out of suspects yet.

I just needed to find Gregory Garland.

Would he be Lionel's next of kin?

CHAPTER FOURTEEN

With Evelyn out of the golf cart, I pulled up in front of the old brick building where Diffy Delk's law office was located, I couldn't help but chuckle to myself. Only in Holiday Junction would the town's most eccentric lawyer work out of a building that looked like it hadn't seen a renovation since the 1950s, wearing a polyester suit and all. And then, of course, there was Dave the Rooster.

I'd barely turned off Mama's golf cart when I heard the unmistakable crow of Dave, a sound that had become oddly familiar since I'd first met the bird. He was more of a local character than most people in town, and from what I'd heard, he had quite the fanbase. I couldn't say I wasn't slightly charmed by him either, though I didn't care much for the idea of him sitting on Diffy's desk like some feathered secretary.

But Dave did have his own job as a security guard at the airport—kinda like one of those police sniffing dogs.

I pushed open the door, the familiar creak of the old hinges echoing through the narrow hallway. Inside, the place smelled like mothballs and old books, fitting for someone like Diffy who seemed to live permanently stuck in the past.

I stepped over the threshold to his office, the warmth of the room a welcome contrast to the biting chill outside. There sat Diffy, perched behind his oversized oak desk in that familiar burnt-yellow shirt and brown polyester suit that looked like it came straight out of 1974. He was leaning back, sipping from a mug that I highly suspected was filled with spiked eggnog. And there, perched in the corner on his own little platform, was Dave, his beady eyes fixed on me as if daring me to make a move.

"Violet Rhinehammer!" Diffy bellowed, his grin wide and welcoming. "What brings you to my humble office? Or did you stop by to see Darren? Or Dave? He runs the place more than I do." He pointed his thumb toward the rooster, who let out a soft cluck in response. "What can ole Diffy do for you?"

I smiled politely, casting a glance at the second cup of eggnog sitting beside Dave's perch. "Diffy, I am looking for Darren," I said, glancing around. "Is he here?"

"Well, you're in luck!" He leaned forward, pushing his eggnog aside and clasping his hands together. "Darren's been busy lately. Took his client to the bar for a little... consultation, if you know what I mean."

"So he's not here?" I asked, keeping my tone light but purposeful.

Diffy leaned back, swirling the eggnog in his mug as if weighing his options.

After a moment, he gave me a sly grin and said, "Nope. Took Gregory Garland to the Jiggle Joint."

The name hit me like a ton of bricks.

"Gregory Garland?" I repeated, trying to keep my voice steady. "Why would he need a lawyer?" I asked in the hopes Diffy's lips were loose after drinking a little too much eggnog.

Diffy shrugged, taking a long sip of his eggnog. "That's a good question, isn't it? Family business, I imagine, now that his brother was murdered and Darren's dad is looking into Gregory as the killer. But you'd have to ask Darren or Gregory himself for the details." Diffy's head jerked back as he belched.

"What do you know about Gregory? I mean, I've heard a little, but I don't know him." I leaned in slightly, my curiosity piqued.

"Well, he's not exactly what you'd call the 'prodigal son.' Or brother. Left town a long time ago and rarely looked back." Diffy scratched his chin thoughtfully. "I'd wager he's not here for the

Christmas festivities, if you catch my drift." He gave me a knowing look.

Before I could ask more, Dave let out a sharp crow, flapping his wings dramatically as if to punctuate Diffy's point.

I glanced at the bird then back at Diffy. "You sure he's not here to claim Lionel's spot as the next of kin?" I asked, my mind racing with possibilities.

"Could be," Diffy said, nodding slowly. "I reckon I better stop drinking this stuff." He downed what was left in his mug before pushing the cup an arm's length away. "You know, client confidentiality and all."

"Yep," I sighed, realizing I wasn't going to get anything else out of him.

"Well, if you need anything else, Violet, you know where to find me. And Dave, of course."

I smiled and stood up, pulling on my coat. "Thanks, Diffy. You've been a big help."

"Anytime, kiddo," he said, leaning back in his chair as I turned to leave. "And if you are ever in the mood for some eggnog, you know where to find me."

"Sure do," I called, shaking my head. "Merry Christmas."

"Merry Christmas," he called out. Dave let out a squawk.

With Diffy and Dave's antics still fresh in my mind, I walked out of the office building and into the crisp December air, my thoughts swirling as fast as the snowflakes falling around me. Gregory Garland, here in town, holed up with Darren at the Jiggle Joint? This day was getting stranger by the minute, and if Gregory was involved in Lionel's death somehow, I needed to know.

I glanced at my phone. I still had some time before lunch with Mama at Freedom Diner. Plenty of time to just "check in" with Darren. I grinned to myself, knowing that was just an excuse to get a look at Gregory. If there was any chance that he was trying to claim Lionel's spot, or worse, involved in his brother's death, I wanted to be one step ahead.

The roads were slick with fresh snow as I made my way through the winding streets of Holiday Junction, the ocean peeking through the gaps between the buildings as I got closer to the coast. The scent of salt water mixed with the ever-present holiday smells of pine and cinnamon filled the air, but my mind was on one thing.

Gregory.

I pulled Mama's golf cart up to the Jiggle Joint and killed the engine. I hopped out, shoving my hands into my coat pockets as I braced myself against the wind coming off the water. The sound of crashing waves could be heard faintly in the distance, but inside the bar, the hum of conversation and clinking glasses would greet me like an old friend.

I pushed open the heavy wooden door, and my eyes immediately adjusted to the dim lighting. The bar was half-full, mostly locals seeking a midday reprieve from their holiday preparations. I scanned the room quickly, my gaze settling at the bar, where I recognized two of my friends.

Shawn and Owen—two barflies that were pretty much always at the Jiggle Joint.

"Easter Bunny." I nodded to Owen, who we referred to as the Easter Bunny. Long story. "Tooth Fairy." I nodded to Shawn. "Merry Christmas, fellows."

Both the men picked up their beers. "Cheers," they yelled when their glasses clinked in the air.

"Where's Darren?" I asked as I looked around the dimly lit bar, not seeing him.

"He came in about an hour ago with Gregory," Owen said, throwing his chin toward a booth in the back.

Darren and Gregory looked like they were having a pretty intense conversation. I couldn't help but wonder if Gregory was seeking legal advice for either something about Lionel's estate, or worse.

Representation for murder.

"Can you do me a favor and tell Darren I popped by on my way to meet Mama at the Freedom Diner?" I asked Owen.

"Sure can," he said and went back to his beer.

The Freedom Diner was just a couple of doors down from the Jiggle Joint. It was buzzing with its usual lunchtime chaos, filled with familiar faces, clinking silverware, and the warm hum of holiday conversation. The scent of frying bacon, cinnamon pancakes, and fresh coffee floated through the air.

I slipped onto one of the stools at the counter, right next to Mama, who already had her hands wrapped around a steaming mug of peppermint hot cocoa. Her oversized scarf, a riot of green and red wool, sat in a tangled heap beside her.

"There you are," Mama said with a wink. "Thought you might've gotten lost chasing a scoop. You hungry?"

"Starving." Grinning, I shed my coat and draped it over the stool next to me.

Nate Lustig, the owner of the diner, waddled over from the griddle with a spatula in hand and his apron dusted in flour. Nate was a solid man, the kind of guy who looked like he could hold his own in a snowstorm without flinching, with a round, ruddy face and a booming laugh that filled any room.

"Well, well, if it isn't the Rhinehammer ladies," Nate said, leaning with his forearm on the counter. "What can I get y'all today?"

"Turkey pot pie," Mama said without missing a beat. "And don't skimp on the crust."

"Same for me," I added, flashing a smile.

"Coming right up." Nate grinned back at me.

He headed back toward the kitchen, but Mama stopped him.

"You've got a minute to sit, Nate?" she asked sweetly, patting the stool on the other side of her.

Nate chuckled, rubbing his hands on his apron before ambling around the counter and hopping up onto the stool with a grunt. "For you, Millie Kay? I've got all the time in the world."

"So," Mama said with a conspiratorial twinkle in her eye, "we were just talking about the lodge. I heard you were pretty impressed with how Darren restored it."

We hadn't even mentioned the lodge since I'd gotten to the diner, but I knew this was Mama's way of getting on with the investigation we'd started at the *Junction Journal*. Mama had a keen sniffer on her. She could find out things that even the best reporter couldn't.

I just let her do her thing.

"Oh yeah," Nate said, nodding enthusiastically. "He did one heck of a job. It looks better than it ever did. Makes you proud to see it standing tall again."

"You knew the lodge back in the day?" I asked, leaning in a bit, curious where this conversation might lead.

"Knew it?" Nate let out a booming laugh. "I was practically raised in that place. Used to help out in the kitchens when I was a kid. And let me tell you, that lodge has seen its fair share of excitement. You ever hear about the old gambling tunnels?"

"Tunnels?" I asked, glancing at Mama, whose brow lifted in interest.

"Yep," Nate said, lowering his voice as if revealing a town secret. "Back in the day, when gambling wasn't exactly legal, they used to run games down in the tunnels beneath the lodge. I was down there once when I was barely old enough to know better. Crumbling walls and creaky boards, probably dangerous, even back then."

"Where exactly were these tunnels?" I pressed, filing the information away in my mind.

"Best I remember, the entrance was off the kitchen pantry. Might be hidden under a floor panel or somethin'." Nate scratched his chin thoughtfully. "Not sure Darren even knows about 'em, though. They'd be pretty tricky to find."

I let that sink in, mentally adding tunnels beneath the lodge to my growing list of things to investigate.

"But let's not dwell on the past," Nate said, shaking his head. "I hear Lionel's death has folks talkin'. Bad business, that."

"Do you think Gregory killed him?" I asked, taking a sip of my water.

"There's been talk." Nate leaned in closer, his voice dropping to a near-whisper. "Folks think Gregory came back for Lionel's estate, but between you and me, Lionel didn't have a penny to his name. He put every dollar he ever made back into that art district project. Lived in a tiny rented cottage, one of Rhett Strickland's places, no less."

"Then why would Gregory show up now?" Mama asked curiously.

"Well..." Nate shrugged, his eyes gleaming with gossip. "Word is, he and Evelyn Frost might be trying to rekindle an old flame. Neither of 'em ever married, you know."

"Oh, now that's interesting," Mama said, her eyes lighting up as she leaned on the counter. "Do tell, Nate. Did they used to be sweet on each other?"

Nate chuckled. "Well, that's just what I heard. Small towns, you know how it goes."

Mama hummed with satisfaction, her eyes sparkling with amusement. "This whole thing just keeps gettin' juicier," Mama said, rubbing her hands together.

I filed away everything Nate had said, my mind racing with new possibilities. If Lionel had no money and Gregory didn't stand to gain anything from his death, then what was his real reason for being in town? Could it really be about Evelyn?

Before I could ask any more questions, the bell above the diner door jingled, and the door swung open with a gust of cold wind.

I glanced over my shoulder, and there stood Darren, his expression grim. His eyes locked on mine, and I knew instantly something had gone wrong.

"Violet," he called, brushing snow from his coat as he strode toward us. His dark hair was damp from the falling snow, and there was a sharpness in his gaze that set my nerves on edge.

"What's wrong?" I asked, standing up from my stool.

He stopped in front of me, his jaw tight. "My father just arrested Gregory Garland." There was a bit of panic in his voice.

I blinked, stunned. "For what?" I asked, even though I could probably make an educated guess.

"They found threatening notes in Lionel's house," Darren said, his voice low. "Notes that were linked back to Gregory."

I exchanged a glance with Mama, whose brow furrowed in concern. "Do you think Gregory's guilty?" she asked.

"No," Darren said firmly, his eyes never leaving mine. "I don't. But we need to get to the station. I'm going to defend him."

Without missing a beat, I grabbed my coat and threw it over my shoulders. Mama reached for her scarf, worry etched into her face.

"Stay here, Mama," I said gently. "I'll call you as soon as I know more."

"Be careful, sugar," she said, her voice tinged with concern. "Take the golf cart."

I gave her a quick nod before turning back to Darren. "Let's go." I hurried behind him.

He held the door open for me, and as we stepped out into the swirling snow, I couldn't help but feel the weight of the situation. Gregory's arrest only raised more questions, and something deep in my gut told me we were far from uncovering the truth.

Darren's jaw was clenched as we climbed into the golf cart, and the heater blasted warm air against our frozen faces. I shot him a glance, knowing representing Gregory wasn't just a professional move for him—this was personal.

"We'll figure this out," I said, squeezing his hand reassuringly.

"We have to," he muttered, shifting the cart into gear and peeling out of the diner parking lot. The snow continued to fall, thick and heavy, as we sped toward the police station.

Deep down, I knew that whatever was waiting for us at that station would reveal only a fraction of the truth about Lionel Garland's murder.

CHAPTER FIFTEEN

Darren pulled Mama's golf cart into the small parking lot outside the Holiday Junction Police Station, the thick snow crunching beneath the tires. Even with the heater humming inside the cab, a chill had settled deep in my bones. The town's police station was a squat brick building with a wooden wreath pinned haphazardly to the front door—the station's attempt at festive cheer.

It didn't exactly scream comfort and joy.

Inside, the fluorescent lights buzzed overhead. Phones rang sporadically, interrupted by the occasional chatter of officers popping in and out of their cubicles. The room smelled faintly of burnt coffee and pine-scented air freshener, likely one of Chief Strickland's attempts to mask the lingering scents of old paper and stale donuts.

Darren marched ahead of me, snowflakes still clinging to his dark hair as he made a beeline for the front desk. I followed, brushing snow off my coat and stomping my boots on the mat to shake off the cold.

We barely had time to make it to the counter before a familiar voice chirped out from behind the counter.

"Well, look what the cat dragged in." Fern Banks' voice was unmistakable, sugary sweet, with just enough bite to make you think twice.

She emerged from behind a desk wearing a tight police-issued jacket over a shimmering turtleneck that would have looked more at home at a holiday gala than at the police station. Fern was a local legend, or celebrity—however you wanted to put it.

She was a former beauty queen who'd somehow decided that her second act would be in law enforcement. And, of course, she was dripping in jewelry. Oversized jingle-bell earrings swung with her every step, and her wrists were adorned with at least three glittering charm bracelets. Definitely not normal for a police deputy, but I bet Chief Strickland didn't want to fuss with her about her attire.

"Fern," Darren said with a tight nod, clearly focused on more pressing matters.

"Darren Strickland," Fern sang, propping one manicured hand on her hip, "aren't you looking all business today?"

I stepped up beside Darren. "Fern, what's going on with Gregory Garland?" I asked, no time to play around with her.

"Oh, you're in for a treat." She leaned in, the gold flecks in her eyeshadow catching the overhead lights. She looked directly at Darren and said, "Your daddy arrested Gregory, and things are getting juicy. You know we found some *very* interesting notes over at Lionel Garland's cottage, don't you?"

"What kind of notes?" I asked, my pulse quickening.

"Threatening notes. Found them right in Lionel's things. And the best part? They were linked back to Gregory. Looks like he might've had more than one reason to bump off his brother." Fern's grin widened.

I frowned. "But Lionel didn't have any money. What would Gregory gain from killing him?" I wondered aloud.

Fern gave an exaggerated shrug, her earrings jingling. "People do crazy things for all sorts of reasons. Maybe an old grudge, maybe jealousy? They were brothers, after all. But it's not my job to figure out the *why*, sweetheart. That's what we've got detectives for." She tossed a wink at Darren. "Or lawyers."

I could tell Darren was biting his tongue to keep from snapping at her, and Fern wasn't finished.

"You know," she said, lowering her voice conspiratorially, "they had to get a subpoena to search Lionel's place. And wouldn't you know it, those notes were sitting right there in Gregory's things, clear as day."

"Gregory's things?" I repeated, narrowing my eyes. "That's odd."

"Odd? Or convenient?" Fern said with a smirk, clearly enjoying the gossip.

Before I could press her further, Darren spoke up.

"I need to talk to Gregory." His voice was curt, all business. "I'm his lawyer."

"Oh, of course." Fern gave a playful wave toward the hallway. "He's in interrogation. Right this way, Counselor."

Darren gave me a quick glance before heading down the hall with Fern, leaving me standing near the front desk. I leaned against the counter, my mind racing. Gregory's arrest felt too clean, too easy, and Lionel's murder was anything but.

Just as I was deciding whether to follow Darren, my phone buzzed in my pocket. I pulled it out, glancing at the screen.

Evelyn Frost.

I hesitated a moment before answering. "Hello?" I said.

"Violet, thank God," Evelyn's voice came through the line, low and urgent. "I need to see you. Right away."

"Evelyn, what's going on?" I asked, my heart thudding.

"Please," she said, her tone almost desperate. "Meet me at the lodge, at our booth in the market. I need to explain everything. It's important. It's about Gregory. He is at the police station being arrested for Lionel's murder, and he didn't do it."

I glanced toward the hallway where Darren had disappeared with Fern.

"I'm on my way," I said, ending the call and slipping my phone back into my pocket.

Just as I turned to leave, another text buzzed on my phone. It was from Darren.

Darren: *Hey, sorry I left you in the lobby. Waiting to talk to Gregory. I could be a few. Go on and do what you need to do. How about another date tonight? Dress warm—got something fun planned.*

A small smile tugged at my lips despite the tension in my chest.

Me: *Yes! Can't wait. What time?*

I shot the message back, knowing Darren's idea of a fun date usually involved something cozy and thoughtful.

But first, I had to meet Evelyn. I pulled my coat tighter around me and headed for the door, bracing myself for the cold winter air.

I climbed back into Mama's golf cart. The heater hummed faintly as I steered out of the police station lot and onto the snowy streets. My mind raced as I drove toward the lodge, wondering what secrets Evelyn had been keeping—and why she was so desperate to share them now.

The streets were quieter now, blanketed in snow, the twinkling holiday lights reflecting off the white ground. As I turned up the narrow road leading toward the mountain, I couldn't shake the feeling that the pieces of the puzzle were finally about to come together. But the question was, would I get to the truth before it was too late?

CHAPTER SIXTEEN

The snow fell more heavily as I made my way up the narrow road leading to the lodge. The frosty world outside seemed determined to draw my thoughts away from the puzzle swirling in my mind.

Whatever Evelyn needed to tell me, it had to be important. But before I could find out what she had to say, I needed to check in with Jessica.

The familiar scent of pine hit me the moment I stepped inside the lodge, along with the warm air that melted the chill clinging to my skin.

The fireplace crackled, its golden flames licking the logs, making the room feel like a cozy Christmas postcard. The sounds of soft holiday piano music drifted through the space, the musician playing a medley of cheerful carols from where the piano was stationed near the sitting area.

Couples sat nestled in plaid blankets on deep leather couches, sipping on cocoa from oversized mugs and chatting in low, contented murmurs. The large tree in the center of the lobby was festooned with red bows, delicate snowflake ornaments, and twinkling lights. Its star glimmered at the very top, catching the soft light from the nearby windows, where fresh snow gathered on the sills.

Jessica stood behind the front desk, flipping through the reservation book with one hand, a candy cane hooked over her ear like a pencil. As soon as she spotted me, she perked up, her festive red sweater covered in a tiny reindeer pattern with bells that jingled softly as she moved. "Back already, Violet?" she said with a grin.

"Always," I replied, brushing snow off my coat. "I needed to ask if you've had any unexpected visitors today."

"Oh, you mean Jeffrey and Annalise?" she asked.

"The *Southern Charm* crew?" I raised a brow.

"They've been hanging around all day, sniffing out anything they can find about Lionel's murder." Jessica nodded, her tone taking on a conspiratorial whisper. "Mostly, they were interested in the security footage."

"Did you show it to them?" That piqued my interest.

Jessica smirked, clearly pleased with herself. "Told

them it wasn't public. You know, official police business," she said.

Before I could respond, the lodge doors swung open, letting in a sharp gust of wind, and in walked Jeffrey and Annalise. Snowflakes clung to their coats, and their expressions soured the moment they spotted me.

"There you are!" Jeffrey marched toward me, his voice loud enough to turn a few curious heads.

I stood my ground, bracing myself for the confrontation. "What can I do for you?"

"I want my camera back," Jeffrey demanded, his chest heaving in impatience.

I crossed my arms. "About that... the police have it now. They took the SD card as evidence since your photos were from the night Lionel was killed." I took great pleasure in how my words landed.

Jeffrey's eyes darkened with irritation. "You went through them?" he seethed.

"I did," I answered calmly. "And since they were relevant to the investigation, the police kept the card."

Jeffrey muttered under his breath, tugging Annalise's arm. "We'll see about that," he said, shooting me a glare as they stomped back out into the snow, clearly heading toward the police station.

Jessica chuckled, resting her elbows on the desk.

"Some people just can't handle a little drama, huh?" She laughed.

I shook my head, unable to suppress a smile. "You mentioned the security footage earlier. Mind if I take a look?" I asked.

"Since you are the boss's girlfriend," Jessica said as she beamed, clearly enjoying the unfolding intrigue, "right this way."

She led me down a narrow hallway behind the counter and into a small room with a desk, a computer monitor, and several live feeds from the lodge's security cameras. A garland of pine and tiny ornaments ran along the top of the screen, giving the otherwise utilitarian space a festive touch. Jessica clicked through the footage from the night Lionel died, bringing up the relevant time frame.

I leaned closer to the monitor, scanning the scenes. Guests milled about the booths, setting up their displays, chatting and laughing. The camera caught just the edge of Lionel's booth showed him fussing with his setup, his usual frown plastered on his face. But there was nothing unusual. No suspicious figures loitering near the windows, no one sneaking in or out.

"See?" Jessica tapped her nail against the screen. "We can't see the window. All I know is that Darren made sure we had all the windows locked."

I frowned.

"These old structures don't have a lot of insulation." Her demeanor matched mine.

"So how did the killer get in and out without anyone noticing?" I asked.

Jessica shrugged, her candy cane earring jingling as she moved. "Beats me. Other than Lionel throwing a fit about his booth placement, everything seemed normal," she said.

I filed that information away. If the killer hadn't entered through the windows or doors, how had they managed to commit the crime unnoticed?

"Thanks, Jessica. Let me know if you remember anything else."

"Will do. And I'll keep an eye on those *Southern Charm* folks for you," she said.

I left the security room and weaved through the lobby toward the market stalls. The holiday atmosphere in the lodge felt surreal given the dark mystery lingering beneath the surface. Guests wandered the aisles of the indoor market as they admired handcrafted ornaments and holiday trinkets. Children clutched plush reindeer toys, and the scent of spiced cider filled the air.

I spotted Evelyn at her booth, stirring a cup of cocoa, her expression tight and anxious. I made my way over, my boots clicking softly against the wooden floor. "Evelyn," I greeted, my voice low.

She glanced up, her eyes wary. "Violet. Thank you for coming," she said.

"You said you needed to tell me something?" I asked.

Evelyn glanced around, as if checking for eavesdroppers, then leaned closer. "Gregory and I were at the midnight screening of *It's a Wonderful Life* the night Lionel was killed."

I blinked, surprised. "Together?"

She gave a small nod. "We didn't want anyone to know. We figured the theater was the safest place to talk without being seen. The sweater I had taken back had gotten snagged on the arm of the chair, and sequins went all over. I returned it because I knew I couldn't wear a snagged sweater and gave it to Emily because I know she could probably fix it and resell it. Honestly I had gotten it to wear for the photos of the magazine if I won."

"Why the secrecy?" I asked. "What were you two talking about?"

"Lionel. Gregory and I both received letters." Evelyn's expression darkened. "Threatening ones. They said Lionel had stolen the ornament design he used in the competition."

I inhaled sharply. "Who sent the letters?"

Evelyn shook her head. "We don't know. They

were anonymous, but they warned that if Lionel didn't withdraw the ornament made from the stolen design from the competition, they'd make sure he paid for it," she said.

"And you confronted Lionel about it?"

"Yes. We both did, separately. He brushed me off, told me to mind my business. Gregory got the same treatment."

"So you went to the theater that night to figure out what to do?" I asked, not piecing it together.

"Yes," Evelyn confirmed. "We needed a private place to talk it over. We thought about going to the police, but we wanted to be sure before we made it public."

"And you're sure Gregory was with you the whole time?"

She nodded again. "From the previews to the credits. If you don't believe me, check the theater's cameras."

I exhaled, absorbing the new information. "I believe you," I said, even though I'd make sure the camera footage was followed up on.

Evelyn relaxed, though the tension in her shoulders didn't fully leave. "Thank you, Violet. I know how it must look, but Gregory didn't kill Lionel. He's innocent."

I gave her a small, reassuring smile. "I'll look into it."

Evelyn nodded, a flicker of hope in her eyes, and turned back to her booth. As I made my way toward the lodge's exit, my thoughts churned. Gregory and Evelyn had alibis, and the threatening letters suggested someone else had a motive.

A motive tied to a stolen design.

But who?

As I turned on the ignition of Mama's golf cart and the heater hummed to life, I stared out at the snow-covered road ahead. With each passing moment, the puzzle grew more complicated. There were no solid suspects now.

Not yet.

CHAPTER SEVENTEEN

Instead of driving all the way back to the office, I had called Mama to see if I could keep the golf cart overnight. I would finish tomorrow's online newspaper at home.

The cart heater buzzed as I drove home through the falling snow, the streets aglow from the holiday lights that wrapped around every lamppost and tree. It wasn't a long ride, and soon enough, I parked the cart out front, climbed the steps to my place, and settled into the warmth of my little apartment.

I kicked off my boots, hung up my coat, and poured myself a cup of cocoa. There were still a couple of hours before Darren was due to pick me up for our date, so I curled up on the couch with my laptop, eager to upload the photos I'd taken at the Christmas Market.

Going through the photos was more fun than I expected. Each picture seemed to capture a perfect holiday moment—families laughing, kids bundled in bright scarves and holding oversized mugs of cocoa, and booths filled with handmade ornaments and garlands. There were so many good ones, it was hard to narrow them down.

I smiled as I edited, adding a few captions in my head: "Holiday Junction in All Its Christmas Glory," or maybe "A Market Full of Cheer—Until the Icicles Start Falling." I snickered at the last one I came up with but decided to simply go with "Market Full of Cheer" for the headline.

After selecting my top picks, I set the laptop aside and pulled my notebook onto my lap, flipping to a fresh page.

I uncapped my pen and started jotting down the pieces of the mystery I had so far, hoping that putting everything on paper would help me find the missing connection.

I wrote "The Letters" as the header and began to write down everything I could.

Evelyn and Gregory had both received anonymous letters, each warning them that Lionel had stolen the design for his winning ornament. Whoever sent the letters wasn't subtle. They wanted Lionel to stop using the design, and if he didn't, they threatened to make him "pay." The phrasing was blunt enough to suggest the sender wasn't bluffing, and now that Lionel was dead, it felt like more than just an idle threat.

What I didn't know yet was who sent the letters or how the sender knew about the design in the first place. Whoever it was, they knew enough to stir up trouble between Lionel and anyone connected to him. Evelyn and Gregory both seemed rattled by the accusations—enough that they confronted Lionel separately.

Next, I wrote the heading "Confrontations with Lionel."

Both Evelyn and Gregory admitted to arguing with Lionel about the design. Evelyn said she tried to get him to come clean, but Lionel had brushed her off, telling her to "mind her own business." Gregory, from what I could gather, didn't take the brush-off quite as well. Their conversation had escalated into a full-blown argument, though I didn't have the details yet.

The arguments were certainly tense, but neither Evelyn nor Gregory seemed eager to confess to anything more. They both claimed their frustrations ended with words—nothing more.

Then I wrote down "ALIBIS" in capital letters.

Both Evelyn and Gregory swore they were together the night Lionel was killed, tucked away in the dark theater for the midnight screening of *It's a Won-*

derful Life. Evelyn insisted they'd chosen the theater because it was a quiet place where no one would see them talking. That felt like an odd detail to throw in. Were they hiding something beyond the contents of the letters?

Either way, their alibi seemed solid. And the theater's CCTV footage would backed up their story, showing both of them in the theater for the entire runtime of the movie. Which would rule them out as suspects.

Or did it?

I drummed my pen against the notebook, underlining the word "Motive?" at the top of the page.

Both Evelyn and Gregory had a reason to want Lionel out of the way—if they believed he'd stolen the design, that is. But they'd both denied wanting him dead. Still, the letters suggested someone else had a motive strong enough to act.

And what would either Evelyn or Gregory gain by killing Lionel, anyway? From everything I'd heard, Lionel didn't have much to leave behind. Nate Lustig had told me that every cent Lionel made went straight back into renovating the art district. Lionel had even been living modestly in a rented cottage, courtesy of Rhett Strickland. There wasn't some hidden fortune waiting to be inherited, and it was hard to imagine someone killing for an estate that didn't exist.

What about Gregory?

My pen hovered over Gregory's name on the page. He was still a puzzle.

According to Nate, Gregory had been gone from Holiday Junction for years, only to reappear around the time of his brother's death. Nate had speculated—rather gleefully—that Gregory might've come back to rekindle something with Evelyn. It was gossip, sure, but gossip often held a sliver of truth.

The question was, if Gregory didn't return for Evelyn—and he certainly didn't come back to inherit anything from Lionel—then why was he here? Was there more to his argument with Lionel than he and Evelyn were letting on?

I leaned back against the couch, my notebook resting on my knee as I stared out the window, lost in thought. Snowflakes swirled beyond the glass, each one catching the glow from the nearby streetlights, twinkling like miniature stars.

The sudden knock at the door jolted me upright, nearly scaring me half to death. I placed the notebook on the coffee table and made my way to the door, my heart fluttering with both anticipation and excitement.

When I swung it open, there stood Darren, snow dusting his dark hair and that familiar grin warming his face.

He wore a thick wool coat, the kind that looked as

though it had fought through more than one winter storm, and a plaid scarf was draped casually around his neck. The sight of him standing there with snowflakes in his hair and his smile all for me sent a warm flutter through my chest.

"Ready to go?" he asked as he brushed snow off his coat.

"Absolutely." I grabbed my coat and scarf then pulled the door closed behind me as we headed down the front steps. I gave him a teasing look. "So, where exactly are we going?"

"This way," he said, gesturing toward the road that led in the direction of the lodge.

"On foot?" I asked, raising an eyebrow. "I've got Mama's golf cart. It even has heat."

"On foot," he insisted, wrapping his arm around my shoulders. The warmth of him spread over me like a cozy blanket, and I leaned into him, matching his stride as the snow crunched beneath our boots.

"Alright, but if we freeze, I'm blaming you," I teased, nudging him gently with my shoulder.

He chuckled, squeezing me tighter against him. "I promise you'll love it."

The night was beautiful. The snow glittered beneath the soft glow of Christmas lights strung along storefronts and draped over lampposts. Icicle lights hung from rooflines, glowing white and blue, and a carol drifted on the breeze as we passed a group of bundled-up singers stationed at the corner of the art district.

We didn't talk about Lionel's murder or the investigation. This was a moment just for us.

A slice of holiday magic in the middle of all the chaos.

The tension I hadn't realized I was carrying in my shoulders started to melt away, bit by bit, with every step we took.

By the time we reached the edge of the Christmas tree farm, the world around us had transformed into a wintry dreamland. Rows of evergreens stretched as far as the eye could see, their branches heavy with freshly fallen snow. Strings of warm yellow lights crisscrossed above the path, casting a soft glow over the trees and the families wandering between them, searching for the perfect one.

Near the entrance, a roaring fire crackled inside a stone firepit, sending waves of heat into the crisp night air. A booth nearby served mulled cider in steaming cups, and I breathed deeply to savor the mingled scent of cinnamon and cloves. Carolers in Victorian costumes strolled along the paths, their voices carrying old, familiar tunes.

"This," I whispered, "is perfect."

Darren grinned, clearly pleased with himself. "Told you."

We stopped by the booth for two ciders, wrapping

our hands around the warm cups as we wandered down the rows of trees.

The night felt timeless.

Everything aglow and peaceful, the only sound the crunch of our boots in the snow and the soft hum of Christmas carols in the background.

We bantered back and forth as we strolled, playfully arguing over which tree would be the best fit for my apartment.

"This one's too short," I said, shaking my head at Darren's first suggestion.

"It's not short; it's compact," he argued, running his hand over the snow-dusted branches.

"Compact isn't festive," I teased, nudging him with my shoulder.

"Fine. What about this one?" He gestured toward a towering pine, its branches thick and full.

I tilted my head, pretending to consider it. "If I had a ten-foot ceiling, maybe." I laughed.

"You're impossible." Darren let out a mock sigh of defeat.

"I have high standards," I said with a grin. "This is serious business."

Finally, we found the perfect tree.

A Fraser fir with just the right height and fullness. Darren gave me a triumphant grin as he hauled it over his shoulder.

"This is the one, is it?" he confirmed.

We carried it together toward the booth where we'd seen nets and twine.

After he paid for the tree and a few decorations, we walked hand in hand while Darren dragged the fir behind us, stumbling and laughing through the snow.

Back inside, the tree stood proudly in the corner of my living room, its branches still dusted with snow. Darren shrugged off his coat and rubbed his hands together for warmth as I dug out the ornaments we'd bought at the farm.

"Ready for the fun part?" I asked, holding up a string of lights.

Darren grinned. "I thought picking out the tree was the fun part."

"Nope. This is the fun part." I tossed him one end of the lights, and we began winding them around the branches, our hands brushing occasionally as we worked side by side. Each time our fingers touched, a little spark of something warm and wonderful shot through me.

Once the lights were up, we began hanging the ornaments—wooden snowflakes, glittering balls, and candy canes. Darren made a big show of trying to arrange them all in a straight line.

"That's not how you decorate a tree." I laughed, nudging him with my shoulder.

"Oh? And what's the proper method, according to

the expert?" he teased, moving a candy cane an inch to the left.

"It's all about balance, obviously." I stood on my tiptoes to hang a snowflake on a high branch.

"Obviously." He gave me a playful grin, his eyes sparkling in the soft glow of the lights.

By the time the last ornament was in place, the tree looked beautiful. Its lights twinkled softly, reflecting off the glass ornaments. We stood back, admiring our handiwork.

"It's perfect," I whispered.

"So are you," Darren murmured, his voice low and warm.

Before I could respond, he leaned in, his lips brushing mine in a kiss that was soft and slow, the kind that made my heart race and the world melt away. I kissed him back, savoring the moment, the warmth of his arms, and the scent of pine filling the space around us.

We curled up on the couch afterward. Darren had poured us two glasses of wine, and we sat there admiring the tree. The lights bathed the room in a warm, cozy light, and for the first time in what felt like days, I let myself relax.

As we sat there, Darren shifted beside me, his eyes lighting up as if he'd just remembered something.

"You know, Nate mentioned those old tunnels

under the lodge," I said. "The ones used for illegal gambling?"

"I'd completely forgotten about them when I bought the place," Darren said, setting his wine glass down. "I wonder if they might still be there."

"Nate thought the entrance was in the kitchen pantry," I said. "Do you think they're still accessible?" A thrill of excitement shot through me.

"Only one way to find out," he said, as if he were reading my mind.

We exchanged a look, the same look we always shared when we were about to do something a little crazy.

"Want to go check it out?" I asked, already knowing the answer.

"Absolutely." Darren stood, grabbing his coat. "Let's bundle up. We've got a lodge to explore."

With a shared grin, we bundled up in our coats and scarves. The snow was still falling softly as we stepped outside, ready to uncover whatever secrets the lodge, and its hidden tunnels, might hold.

This time, we did take Mama's golf cart.

CHAPTER EIGHTEEN

Even at night, the lodge was alive with festive charm. Warm lights glowed from the windows, and the faint hum of holiday music drifted out into the cold night air. A few late-night guests still roamed the grounds, bundled in scarves and chatting in low voices as they sipped cocoa under the soft glow of the outdoor heaters.

We didn't have to sneak in—Darren owned the place, after all—but there was still an air of excitement as we pushed through the front doors. The warmth of the lobby embraced us like a cozy blanket, and the familiar scents of pine and cinnamon filled the space. The large fireplace crackled in the far corner, casting flickering shadows over the stone walls.

"Jessica's not at the desk," I whispered, my eyes scanning the dimly lit lobby.

"It's her night off," Darren murmured, tugging me gently toward the hallway that led to the kitchen. "Come on."

We moved quickly through the lodge, our footsteps muffled by the thick, plush carpet. Decorations twinkled in the low light—garlands draped over banisters, wreaths hung on every door, and strings of tiny lights wrapped around the wooden beams above us. It was as if the entire lodge was holding its breath, waiting for Christmas to arrive.

When we reached the kitchen, Darren flicked on the overhead light, revealing a pristine space filled with gleaming countertops and rows of neatly stacked pots and pans. The scent of baked goods lingered in the air, as if the kitchen had been hard at work all day preparing for the guests.

"This way," Darren said, leading me to the far corner, where the pantry door stood slightly ajar.

The pantry was a narrow space lined with shelves stocked with everything from canned goods to jars of spices. Darren ran his hand along the floor, feeling for the hidden panel Nate had mentioned.

"Got it," he whispered triumphantly as his fingers brushed over a faint seam in the tiles.

The panel lifted with a soft groan, revealing a set of wooden steps descending into darkness. A musty scent of damp earth and old wood wafted up from below. I shivered, pulling my coat tighter around me.

"Ladies first?" Darren teased, holding out his hand.

I rolled my eyes but took his hand as I carefully descended the steps. My phone's flashlight cut through the darkness, illuminating the narrow tunnel below. The walls were made of rough stone, and the ceiling was low enough that Darren had to duck his head as we made our way deeper into the tunnel.

The air was cool and damp, and our footsteps echoed eerily in the confined space. It felt like we were stepping back in time, into a place forgotten by the modern world. The deeper we went, the darker it became, the only sound the occasional drip of water from the stone ceiling above.

"Creepy," I muttered, my breath visible in the cold air.

"Admit it," Darren said from behind me. "You love it."

I gave a reluctant smile. "Maybe a little."

We continued down the tunnel, our phones lighting the way. After a few more steps, we stumbled upon a stack of old crates covered in dust and cobwebs.

I crouched down and brushed away the grime to reveal a collection of old photographs and yellowed papers. "Look at this," I whispered, holding up a faded photograph of a group of men seated around a poker table, stacks of chips and cards spread out before them.

Darren knelt beside me, his breath warm against my cheek as he peered at the photo. "That's gotta be from the old gambling days."

We sifted through the papers and photos, uncovering what looked like blueprints and sketches. My heart skipped a beat when I pulled out a drawing of an intricate ornament nearly identical to Lionel's winning design.

"This is it," I whispered, holding the sketch up for Darren to see. "Lionel's ornament."

Darren leaned closer, his expression darkening. "He really did steal the design."

We stared at the drawing in silence, the weight of the discovery settling between us. Lionel hadn't just borrowed inspiration—he'd stolen the design outright, passing it off as his own. And whoever had created this original design had been left in the shadows.

Before either of us said anything else, the soft scuff of footsteps echoed from the tunnel behind us.

I froze, my heart hammering in my chest. Darren's phone light swept the tunnel behind us, illuminating the narrow path.

And then, out of the shadows, a figure stepped forward.

Jessica.

Her face was pale, her eyes sharp, and in her hand, she held a gun.

Its barrel gleamed in the dim light.

"He sure did," Jessica said, her voice steady and cold. "And he paid for it."

CHAPTER NINETEEN

Jessica's knuckles whitened as she gripped the gun tighter. Her eyes were wild but focused, gleaming in the dim light of our phone flashlights. She took a step closer, her breath steady despite the tension crackling in the stale air around us. My pulse pounded in my ears, but I kept my face calm, locking eyes with her.

"You want to know why?" Jessica's voice was sharp, her words brittle, like she'd been holding this secret for too long and it had finally splintered. "That ornament design—it wasn't just some idea Lionel borrowed. It belonged to my family."

Darren shifted beside me, his body tense, ready to move. I could feel the heat radiating off him despite the chill of the tunnel. I inched my hand into my pocket, fingers brushing against my phone, trying to think of anything that might help us out of this.

Jessica kept the gun leveled at us, her lips curling into a bitter smile. "Years ago, that design belonged to my great-uncle. It was a family treasure. When I saw the contest, I thought it would be a perfect way to honor his memory. Lionel was supposed to help me—said he'd enter it for me since I didn't have the connections. I trusted him." Her voice cracked, just a hairline fracture of pain slipping through. "But instead, that snake entered it himself and slapped his name on it like it was his idea all along."

I exchanged a quick glance with Darren, who gave a small, almost imperceptible nod. We were on the same page—stall her, keep her talking, find an opening.

"When I realized what he'd done," Jessica continued, her tone sharpening, "I didn't know what to do. I thought Evelyn or Gregory might put a stop to it, so I sent them letters, warning them about Lionel. But neither of them did anything."

"So you confronted Lionel yourself," I said softly, drawing her focus back to me.

Jessica's grip tightened on the gun. "That's right. We had it out, right there at the lodge the night of the festival. Everyone thought he was fussing over his booth placement. But we were arguing about *my* design."

Her eyes gleamed with fury, her breath coming faster now. "He looked me in the eye and told me I was a nobody, that no one would care where the design came from. And I just... snapped."

She exhaled, her voice taking on a chilling calm. "The icicles outside the window gave me the perfect idea. I knew the CCTV cameras wouldn't catch me if I escaped through the tunnels. So I waited until the right moment, climbed in through the window... and stabbed him."

My stomach twisted, the cold truth settling over me like a heavy blanket.

Jessica's voice hardened. "He didn't even see it coming. One sharp jab, and that was it. The icicle melted. No evidence. No weapon."

Her finger twitched against the trigger, and I felt Darren tense beside me, ready to act.

"But now," Jessica continued, her smile turning predatory, "I've got a problem. You two know too much."

She stepped closer, her eyes narrowing. "I could leave you down here. No one will hear the shots from this deep. By the time they find your bodies, I'll be long gone."

The cold weight of her words settled over the tunnel, and for a moment, everything stood still.

Then Darren spoke, his voice low and steady. "Jessica, listen to me." He kept his hands raised, his expression calm and earnest. "You don't want to do this. Killing us isn't going to fix what Lionel did to you."

Jessica's laugh was sharp, bitter. "It'll fix the problem of you knowing what I did."

"Will it, though?" Darren asked, taking a small step forward, drawing her focus. "Think about it. You've gone this far without anyone suspecting you. Do you really want to throw it all away now? If you kill us, you're not going to walk away free. They'll catch you, Jessica. You know they will."

I saw the flicker of doubt cross her face, just a flash of hesitation. It was all we needed.

Darren lunged and grabbed Jessica's arm just as the gun went off, the deafening crack ricocheting off of the tunnel walls. I ducked, my heart slamming against my ribs, and the bullet hit the stone behind me, sending a shower of dust into the air.

Jessica twisted, fighting back, but Darren held fast, his quick reflexes surprising even me. I surged forward, grabbed her other arm, and wrenched the gun away. It clattered to the ground, the sound echoing like a death knell in the narrow space.

Jessica kicked and fought, snarling like a cornered animal, but Darren and I worked together, pinning her arms behind her back. She thrashed, her breath coming in ragged gasps as she tried to free herself, but Darren was stronger.

"You're done, Jessica," Darren said, his voice firm but not unkind. "It's over."

Jessica sagged, the fight draining out of her as the reality of her situation sank in. I grabbed my phone, and my fingers shook as I dialed Chief Strickland's number.

"We've got her," I whispered into the phone, my heart pounding. "She confessed."

Jessica slumped against the wall, her head hanging low. Darren kept his grip on her, steady and unyielding, as we waited for help to arrive. The tension in the tunnel finally began to ease, like a long-held breath being released into the cold night air.

"Why?" I asked quietly, looking at Jessica. "Why didn't you just tell the truth?"

Jessica's eyes, now dull and lifeless, flicked up to meet mine. "Because no one listens to nobodies, Violet. Not unless you make them."

CHAPTER TWENTY

The morning after Jessica's arrest, the news spread through Holiday Junction faster than a snowstorm on Christmas Eve. Everyone had been buzzing about the mystery of Lionel's death for days, and now the truth had finally come out.

Jessica confessed everything in the end about how she had trusted Lionel with her family's cherished ornament design only for him to steal it and enter it into the contest as his own. When her letters to Evelyn and Gregory didn't stop Lionel, she took matters into her own hands—she hid in the tunnels beneath the lodge, slipped in through the window, and used an icicle to end his life.

The chief had been quick to take her into custody, his brow furrowed deep with disappointment, but he offered me and Darren a grateful smile when we gave our statements. Darren stood at my side the whole time, his hand warm and reassuring against the small of my back. It felt good to know we'd solved the mystery.

Together.

Evelyn and Gregory were officially cleared of suspicion, though Evelyn had given me a stern look that said, *"You owe me for that little investigation stunt."* I knew she'd come around.

Gregory, for his part, seemed relieved to have the cloud of suspicion lifted. Maybe, just maybe, he'd stick around town a little longer. After all, Evelyn hadn't pushed him away.

Even Jeffrey and Annalise had decided not to report on the murder, leaving it to me.

I had just enough time to write the full story for the *Junction Journal*'s holiday edition. My fingers flew over the keyboard, recounting the twists and turns, the clues and suspects, and the satisfying resolution that came just in time for the Christmas celebrations. I ended the article on a high note, reminding readers that, even in the most unexpected moments, holiday magic, and justice, had a way of making things right.

With the story sent off and the sun dipping low in the sky, Darren swung by my apartment to escort me to the Christmas tree lighting.

"Come on," he said with a grin, leaning against the doorway, his breath warm against the cold air. "We've got a tree to light, and it won't wait all night. After all, the Merry Maker did pick that spot this year."

I slipped into my coat, scarf, and mittens and grabbed his hand with a smile.

"I wouldn't miss it for the world," I said.

The Christmas Lodge looked a lot different without a murder looming.

Carolers stood at the base of the tree, their voices harmonizing in a rendition of "Silent Night" that made my heart swell. Children ran around the booths, and people sipped steaming cups of mulled cider, their cheeks rosy from the cold outside.

Darren and I found a spot near the front, just as Kristine climbed onto a little platform with a microphone, Mayor Paisley by her side.

"All right, folks," Kristine boomed, her voice carrying through the chilly night air. "It's time. Let's light this tree and kick off the holiday season the right way."

The crowd cheered, and I felt Darren's hand slip into mine, his fingers curling around mine in a way that felt perfectly, undeniably right. I glanced up at him, and he smiled down at me, his eyes crinkling at the corners.

"Think we'll get a quiet Christmas after this?" I teased, nudging him lightly.

"Not a chance. But I'm good with that. Long as I get to spend it with you," he said.

Before I could respond, the mayor gave the signal by yipping, and the massive tree sprang to life, twinkling with thousands of lights in every color imaginable.

The crowd erupted into applause, children squealed with delight, and the carolers launched into "Joy to the World."

I looked up at the tree, feeling the warmth of the moment settle deep into my bones. It was more than just a holiday tradition.

It was a reminder that, no matter how complicated things got, there was always light to be found.

Mama and Daddy stood next to us.

Darren gave my hand a little squeeze, drawing my attention back to him. "Merry Christmas, Violet," he said softly.

"Merry Christmas," I whispered, standing on my tiptoes to kiss him. His lips were warm against mine, and for a moment, everything else fell away—the cold in my bones, the crowd, the chaos of the last few days. It was just us, wrapped in the magic of the season.

When we pulled away, I rested my head against his shoulder, watching the tree sparkle in the night. Around us, Holiday Junction buzzed with life, the town coming together in a way that only happened during the holidays.

And as I stood there with Darren, his arm around

me, I knew that whatever challenges came next, whether it was solving another mystery or just getting through the winter, I'd be ready. Because, just like the holiday lights twinkling in our little village, life had a way of shining brightest in the darkest moments.

CHAPTER TWENTY-ONE

A Note from The Merry Maker
Ho, ho, ho, dear friends!
What a merry little adventure this holiday season turned out to be! I must say, I was tickled peppermint pink to see so many familiar faces—villagers and tourists alike—gathering at the lodge for this year's Christmas tree lighting. And wasn't it the *perfect* spot? Why, I knew from the start that the lodge's grand view of Holiday Junction, dusted in snow and draped in twinkling lights, would make for a holiday celebration no one would soon forget. (And thankfully, no more icicle incidents to disrupt the festivities!)

Carolers filled the air with joyful tunes, mugs of piping hot cider were shared under a blanket of stars, and everything about the night glimmered with that extra sprinkle of magic—just how I like it. I hope you felt the warmth of the season as deeply as I did, from the glow of the tree to the bonds of friendship, family, and—oh yes—just a hint of romance.

It seems love is in the air here in Holiday Junction, too. I wouldn't be surprised if our favorite village lawyer and sharp-witted journalist found themselves cozied up under the mistletoe more than once this season. Could their sparks be as bright as the ones flying off the tree's twinkling lights? Only time will tell, but I'd say this budding romance has all the ingredients for a happily ever after, just like a warm gingerbread cookie fresh from the oven.

Of course, every season must come to a close, but don't you worry your jingle bells—this Merry Maker is always one step ahead, planning something special for the next big celebration. There's always a bit of mischief, mystery, and magic waiting just around the corner. Keep your eyes peeled and your hearts light because you never know when the next Merry Maker sign will pop up—leading you straight into the heart of the holiday fun.

Until next time, keep the spirit bright, the mistletoe ready, and your stockings hung with care... because the next holiday is always closer than you think.

Wishing you joy, peace, and just the right amount of snow,

The Merry Maker

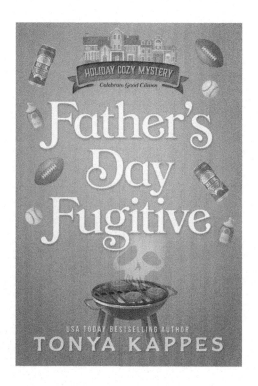

The holiday magic in Holiday Junction may be winding down, but the sleuthing fun is far from over!

Ready to fire up the grill? Preorder the next sizzling installment in the Holiday Junction Mystery series, *Father's Day Fugitive*! Join Violet Rhinehammer as she navigates a BBQ contest gone dangerously wrong, uncovering secrets as tangled as a plate of ribs. Can Violet crack the case, or will this mystery leave her burned?

Continue your stay in Holiday Junction and order *Father's Day Fugitive* now!

BOOKS BY TONYA
SOUTHERN HOSPITALITY WITH A SMIDGEN OF HOMICIDE

Camper & Criminals Cozy Mystery Series

All is good in the camper-hood until a dead body shows up in the woods.

BEACHES, BUNGALOWS, AND BURGLARIES
DESERTS, DRIVING, & DERELICTS
FORESTS, FISHING, & FORGERY
CHRISTMAS, CRIMINALS, AND CAMPERS
MOTORHOMES, MAPS, & MURDER
CANYONS, CARAVANS, & CADAVERS
HITCHES, HIDEOUTS, & HOMICIDES
ASSAILANTS, ASPHALT & ALIBIS
VALLEYS, VEHICLES & VICTIMS
SUNSETS, SABBATICAL AND SCANDAL
TENTS, TRAILS AND TURMOIL
KICKBACKS, KAYAKS, AND KIDNAPPING
GEAR, GRILLS & GUNS
EGGNOG, EXTORTION, AND EVERGREEN
ROPES, RIDDLES, & ROBBERIES
PADDLERS, PROMISES & POISON
INSECTS, IVY, & INVESTIGATIONS

BOOKS BY TONYA

OUTDOORS, OARS, & OATH
WILDLIFE, WARRANTS, & WEAPONS
BLOSSOMS, BBQ, & BLACKMAIL
LANTERNS, LAKES, & LARCENY
JACKETS, JACK-O-LANTERN, & JUSTICE
SANTA, SUNRISES, & SUSPICIONS
VISTAS, VICES, & VALENTINES
ADVENTURE, ABDUCTION, & ARREST
RANGERS, RVS, & REVENGE
CAMPFIRES, COURAGE & CONVICTS
TRAPPING, TURKEY & THANKSGIVING
GIFTS, GLAMPING & GLOCKS
ZONING, ZEALOTS, & ZIPLINES
HAMMOCKS, HANDGUNS, & HEARSAY
QUESTIONS, QUARRELS, & QUANDARY
WITNESS, WOODS, & WEDDING
ELVES, EVERGREENS, & EVIDENCE
MOONLIGHT, MARSHMALLOWS, & MANSLAUGHTER
BONFIRE, BACKPACKS, & BRAWLS

Killer Coffee Cozy Mystery Series

Welcome to the Bean Hive Coffee Shop where the gossip is just as hot as the coffee.

SCENE OF THE GRIND

BOOKS BY TONYA

MOCHA AND MURDER
FRESHLY GROUND MURDER
COLD BLOODED BREW
DECAFFEINATED SCANDAL
A KILLER LATTE
HOLIDAY ROAST MORTEM
DEAD TO THE LAST DROP
A CHARMING BLEND NOVELLA (CROSSOVER WITH MAGICAL CURES MYSTERY)
FROTHY FOUL PLAY
SPOONFUL OF MURDER
BARISTA BUMP-OFF
CAPPUCCINO CRIMINAL
MACCHIATO MURDER
POUR-OVER PREDICAMENT
ICE COFFEE CORRUPTION

Holiday Cozy Mystery Series

CELEBRATE GOOD CRIMES!

FOUR LEAF FELONY
MOTHER'S DAY MURDER
A HALLOWEEN HOMICIDE
NEW YEAR NUISANCE
CHOCOLATE BUNNY BETRAYAL
FOURTH OF JULY FORGERY

SANTA CLAUSE SURPRISE
APRIL FOOL'S ALIBI

Kenni Lowry Mystery Series

Mysteries so delicious it'll make your mouth water and leave you hankerin' for more.

FIXIN' TO DIE
SOUTHERN FRIED
AX TO GRIND
SIX FEET UNDER
DEAD AS A DOORNAIL
TANGLED UP IN TINSEL
DIGGIN' UP DIRT
BLOWIN' UP A MURDER
HEAVENS TO BRIBERY

Magical Cures Mystery Series

Welcome to Whispering Falls where magic and mystery collide.

A CHARMING CRIME
A CHARMING CURE
A CHARMING POTION (novella)
A CHARMING WISH
A CHARMING SPELL

BOOKS BY TONYA

A CHARMING MAGIC
A CHARMING SECRET
A CHARMING CHRISTMAS (novella)
A CHARMING FATALITY
A CHARMING DEATH (novella)
A CHARMING GHOST
A CHARMING HEX
A CHARMING VOODOO
A CHARMING CORPSE
A CHARMING MISFORTUNE
A CHARMING BLEND (CROSSOVER WITH A KILLER COFFEE COZY)
A CHARMING DECEPTION

Mail Carrier Cozy Mystery Series

Welcome to Sugar Creek Gap where more than the mail is being delivered.

STAMPED OUT
ADDRESS FOR MURDER
ALL SHE WROTE
RETURN TO SENDER
FIRST CLASS KILLER
POST MORTEM
DEADLY DELIVERY
RED LETTER SLAY

BOOKS BY TONYA

Maisie Doss Mystery

SLEIGHT OF HAND
TANGLED LIES
GRAVE DECEPTION

About Tonya

Tonya has written over 100 novels, all of which have graced numerous bestseller lists, including the USA Today. Best known for stories charged with emotion and humor and filled with flawed characters, her novels have garnered reader praise and glowing critical reviews. She lives with her husband and a very spoiled rescue cat named Ro. Tonya grew up in the small southern Kentucky town of Nicholasville. Now that her four boys are grown men, Tonya writes full-time in her camper she calls her SHAMPER (she-camper).

Join my newsletter.
and see all of my books on Amazon.
Find all these links on my website, Tonyakappes.com.

For a full reading order of Tonya Kappes's Novels,
visit www.tonyakappes.com

FACEBOOK
INSTAGRAM
GOODREADS

This book is a work of fiction. The characters, incidents, and dialogue are drawn from the author's imagination and are not to be construed as real. Any resemblance to actual events or persons, living or dead, is entirely coincidental. *Cover artist: Mariah Sinclair: The Cover Vault. Editor Red Adept*

Copyright © 2024 by Tonya Kappes. All rights reserved. Printed in the United States of America. No part of this book may be used or reproduced in any manner whatsoever without written permission except in the case of brief quotations embodied in critical articles and reviews. For information email Tonyakappes@tonyakappes.com